THE DRAUGR

A MIDNIGHT GUNN NOVEL #3

C. L. MONAGHAN

The Draugr
A Midnight Gunn Novel #3

Copyright © 2021 Claire Monaghan
Published by Hudson Indie Ink
www.hudsonindieink.com

The Draugr/C.L. Monaghan – 1st ed.
ISBN-13 - 978-1-913769-75-8

PROLOGUE
JANUARY 6TH 1863

ЯⅡR

The shadows grew long as the dull orange of the sputtering oil lamp dimmed. The heavy silence of the parlour inside Number 13 Little Surrey Street was permeated by the *drip drip* of spilled whisky from atop the cluttered desk and the alcohol-induced snores of one Detective Inspector Arthur Gredge. Constable Rowe regarded his superior with a combination of pity and unease as he surveyed the room. The desk, upon which his boss lay recumbent in blissful ignorance, stank of ink and cheap booze. An empty glass remained clutched in Gredge's right hand, and a half-empty bottle of potent amber liquid—The Rose and Crown's finest, no doubt—lay on its side, expunging its contents onto the unswept floor. The fire in the range was out, and Rowe gagged as the stench of what smelled like three-day old soup hit the back of his throat. Taking the iron pot from the range, his face wrinkling in disgust, he emptied it out the back door, gagging again as the rancid slop spattered on the cobbles outside. It looked, and smelled, like vomit.

"Christ save us," Rowe muttered into the crook of his arm. Back inside the house, he plonked the pot down roughly on the dresser and marched to where Gredge slumped, still snoring. Rowe lay a hand on Gredge's shoulder and shook him gently.

"Boss? It's Rowe. You need to wake up." He shook harder. "Inspector? Wake up!" he shouted.

"Away!" Gredge screeched and flung himself backwards off his chair, landing in a tangle of flailing limbs. He caught the whisky bottle with his arm, causing it to crash to the floor and shatter, eliciting an incoherent scream from the inspector.

"Sir, it's me, Constable Rowe. It's alright. It's just me, see?" Rowe held up his hands, palms out in placation. It unsettled him seeing his boss like this, and it wasn't the first time of late. Gredge hadn't been right since he came back from Scotland.

It took a few moments for the pained expression to fade and the Inspector's breathing to regulate, and as lucidity gradually returned, Gredge shuffled onto his knees and pulled himself to his feet. He cleared his throat and ran a hand through his unkempt hair, before smoothing his bushy moustache. Rowe had the good grace to not let his concern show.

"What are you doing here?"

"Well… the Super sent me to find you," Rowe said. "We've got another case."

"What time is it?" Gredge frowned.

"After eight, sir."

"Couldn't it have waited a half hour? I'm not due in until eight-thirty."

"Eight *p.m.*"

"Oh. Really?" Gredge swept a glance over his rumpled clothes and inhaled deeply. "Must've overslept."

"Mmm," Rowe muttered as he inadvertently glanced at the smashed bottle.

"Hate Mondays," Gredge explained.

"It's erm… Tuesday, sir."

"What?"

Rowe shrugged. "Tuesday."

"Fetch my coat!" Gredge shouted.

"Yes, boss." Rowe looked relived to have somewhere to go. He shot out of the parlour and into the hallway. "I'll wait for you by the door," he called back, graciously giving Arthur a few minutes to collect his thoughts.

Tuesday? How in the hell was it Tuesday?

Arthur Gredge had never missed a day's work in his life thus far. He squeezed his eyes shut, trying to recall the events of the previous few days. He'd had supper at the Rose and Crown early Sunday night. He'd brought a bottle home and then… What? Nothing. His mind drew a blank. No matter how hard he tried, he couldn't recall a damned thing that had happened between then and now.

Down at the docks, a gaggle of people were gathered solemnly around a pile of thick ropes and old canvas that was half hidden behind a wall of wooden shipping crates. Aside from the odd gasp, tut, and shake of a head, no one spoke and no one moved out the way as Gredge approached. He shooed people unceremoniously from his path, before finally shoving his way through the blockade of warm bodies to where two very cold and lifeless ones lay.

"Right. What have we got?" Gredge demanded.

"Two victims between eight and twelve years old, I

reckon. It's hard to tell ages with these poor blighters." Rowe sighed. "I hate it when it's kids."

"Don't we all. Carry on, constable."

"Sir." Rowe nodded. "One male, one female. No obvious signs of injury or cause of death that I can see."

"So, what makes this our investigation?"

"The way the bodies have been displayed, similar to before, with the woman in the park."

"You're right. They could well be connected."

"Or... could be a mercy killing by someone who knew or loved them? Definitely not natural?"

"Are you askin' or tellin' me, Rowe?"

"Tellin'."

"Not bad. You're right about the bodies though. Laid out side by side. Certainly doesn't look right. Not your typical murder. Almost looks like they fell asleep and dropped on the spot, poor buggers. Get some lads to gather evidence. There's a crowd, so chances are someone might've seen somethin'. Who called it in?"

"Couple of women. Burgess got their names."

"Right. Off you go then. You'll never make a good detective with me holdin' your hand."

"Yes, boss." Rowe smiled, failing to hide his enthusiasm.

Gredge stayed with the victims to examine the scene for himself while he waited for Rowe to send in the lads. The young boy, dressed in rags, had dark wavy hair. The girl was blonde and wore a dirty brown dress. Both were barefoot. Their extremities were blue, and the rest of their frail little bodies blended almost perfectly with the freshly fallen snow. There was no blood, no physical injury that he could see. They were just dead. The girl's elf-like face was pinched, like she hadn't eaten in an age, and the boy... The boy was *staring* straight him!

Gredge gasped and stumbled backwards, nearly falling over his own feet and bumping into Constable Burgess.

"Inspector. You alright?" Burgess grunted as he reached out and steadied Gredge.

"The boy he… his eyes."

"What about 'im?" Burgess looked over at the corpse.

"They were open just now," Gredge declared, rather breathless.

Burgess looked again. "Look closed to me, boss."

"No, no. He was lookin'…" Gredge stopped midsentence when he saw the frown cross his colleague's face. He turned reluctantly towards the boy, afraid of what he might see, but Burgess was right. The boy's eyes were firmly shut.

"Where's Rowe?" Gredge asked, his voice gruff and demanding to hide his embarrassment, even though he already knew the whereabouts of his junior.

Burgess waved a hand behind him. "Back there, questioning a witness."

"Mmm. Get this seen to then." Gredge indicated to Burgess with a wave of his hand and walked off, shucking up his coat collar against the chill air and adjusting his hat.

He could see Rowe standing at the far end of the street near a warehouse building with two women. As he drew closer, he could hear their voices. One of the women noticed him approaching. Her eyes widened, and she pointed straight at Gredge, talking very animatedly. Rowe looked back at him, frowning, causing Gredge to halt his steps. The two women, who both now wore horrified expressions, began to back away. Rowe seemed to be appealing to them but to no avail, and within seconds, they had both disappeared into the crowd.

"What was that all about?" Gredge asked when he drew level with Rowe.

"Er…" Rowe replied, scratching his chin. "Um…"

"Well, spit it out then, man. Did they see anything suspicious? Did they see who done it?"

"Mmm. Sort of. I suppose. I dunno." Rowe was stuttering now and looking anywhere but at his boss.

"They either did, or they didn't. So, which was it?" snapped Gredge. When no immediate reply came, Gredge snatched Rowe's notebook from him and began reading the constable's scrawled description from the two witnesses. "Man acting suspicious… Medium build. Long brown coat. Bowler hat… Moustache." His heart froze. He recalled the woman's horrified look, how she'd pointed his way. Surely, she hadn't identified— "*Me?*"

Rowe shrugged then nodded, abashed. "I'm sure it's a mistake, sir. I mean—"

"Well, of course it's a bleedin' mistake, you arse! Go see if you can find them and bring them back here for further questioning." He slammed the notebook into Rowe's chest. Rowe grabbed it and scurried off through the crowd of onlookers to track down his two clearly confused witnesses.

Gredge took off his bowler and ran the back of his hand across his sweating brow. Of course it was a mistake. He'd been nowhere near this area in the past week, and those bodies were no more than a day or two cold. There were plenty of men donning bowlers these days. It was quite the new fashion. It was an easy mistake to make, especially in the dim light. What a waste of time it had been, sending Rowe to question the only two witnesses. He should've done it himself. In fact, he would take it over as soon as Rowe returned with the women.

Glancing back at the bodies, Gredge tugged his moustache. A growing sense of unease itched the recesses of his mind. A flash of an image of the boy with blue eyes, open as before but not the same. He drew his brows together in earnest concentration as the prickle of a memory lay tauntingly just out of reach. If he could just… think.

1

THE BRITISH MUSEUM, LONDON
DECEMBER 2ND 1862

ЯⅡR

"**W**hy am I here?" Gredge bemoaned. He scanned the vast exhibition hall with marked disinterest.

"Because I fancied the company," Midnight Gunn replied. "And because my daughter insisted I extend you an invitation to Christmas dinner."

"A letter would've sufficed."

"Now, Arthur. Knowing Polly as you do, do you think anything other than a personal invitation would have satisfied her?" Midnight cocked an eyebrow and smirked.

"Mmm. Nothin' to do with Rowe and his interfering ways, then, eh?"

"Nothing at all. I have absolutely no idea what you are talking about."

"Mmm," Gredge repeated. "But why a museum? It's not exactly my scene, Midnight. A pint down the pub, now that's somethin' I could've got on board with."

"A bit of culture never did anyone any harm. Besides, I have some business here, and I thought you could maybe help."

"Business?"

"Yes. I recently made a discovery in my attic, and I wanted some help researching its origin. We're here to meet one of the museum's curators."

"Thrillin'," Gredge said, rolling his eyes as he followed Midnight's path between the exhibits. "Is that what's in the bag? Your discovery?"

"It is, indeed."

"Why do I get the feeling I'm not gonna like it?"

"Oh, ye of little faith, Arthur. It's an intriguing artefact, I can assure you. Ah! Here we are."

Midnight came to a stop outside an inconspicuous-looking wooden door with the name E. Bird painted in gold lettering at the centre. He knocked on the door then sat down on the oak settle to wait.

"If you say so." Arthur had barely sat down when the door opened and a short, buxom woman sporting men's breaches and a pile of purple-tinged hair strode confidently out to greet them.

"Lord Gunn? Elldy Bird. A pleasure to meet you. Do come in." She turned and strode straight back into her office, leaving the two men outside slightly aghast.

"Close your mouth, Arthur," Midnight whispered.

"She's a woman!"

"I can see why you're such a successful detective. Your observational skills are second to none. After you."

When they entered the room, they were met with a warm smile and an offer of tea, to which they both agreed. The lavender shortbread biscuits that were served to them as an accompaniment were about the only remotely feminine things in the entire office. In fact, it looked so unlike an office that Midnight could have been forgiven for thinking he was inside the sales room of an old curiosity shop. Every conceivable space was rammed full of unusual antiquities.

"You mentioned in your letter that you needed help identifying an object in your possession, Lord Gunn?" Elldy asked.

"Indeed, I do," Midnight replied. He reached into his bag and extracted a bundle of white linen. Holding it in one hand, he carefully unwrapped the cloth to reveal an intricately carved wooden cube roughly the size of an apple. Handing it to the curator, he said, "I think I recognise the runes. Viking, perhaps? I am unsure about the more complicated ones, but I am curious as to the purpose of it. My library at home is a little lacking in Norse mythology, something I intend to remedy. But in the meantime, I hoped you might shed some light on the matter."

Elldy took the cube in both hands and held it close to her face. Squinting, she turned it slowly so as to carefully examine each side.

"Hmm. It's not an object I have seen before, I'll admit. Very interesting though. You are correct in assuming it is of Nordic origin. I estimate it to be late eleventh, possibly twelfth century, but no later. It's remarkably well preserved. Where on earth did you find it?"

"My attic." Midnight smiled at the shocked look on the curator's face. "My late father was a hoarder and somewhat of a collector of curious objects," he offered by way of explanation, not wanting to admit to the whole truth—that his father had, in fact, been an enthusiast of world mythologies and the occult. "I was having a bit of a clear-out and stumbled across a small chest, well hidden in the rafters. When I managed to unlock it, I found this inside."

"There may be a good reason it was locked away," Elldy said. "See these runes here? These look similar to bind runes —two or more runes combined to represent something else— although I have never seen ones like these before." She paused and turned the cube over in her hands, squinting, trying to make sense of the glyphs carved on it. "In this case, they may be intended as a warning or a binding of some sort."

"What sort of warning?" Gredge asked, his tone not one of interest but of distinct wariness.

"I am not sure at this point. I would need to study it at length. I may be completely off course with my initial assessment. We do have a number of Viking artefacts in storage, many of which haven't been catalogued, I'm afraid. But we do have a good amount of articles in our archives that may be of use." She looked up from the cube and, with a twinkle in her eye, asked her two visitors if they would like to see the archives.

"Indeed, we would!" Midnight said. Gredge rolled his eyes as Midnight turned to him, a delighted expression on his face. "Infinitely more interesting than a pint at the Rose and Crown, wouldn't you say, Arthur?

"That depends on your perspective," Gredge grumbled.

Elldy handed Midnight the cube, and he wrapped it back in its packaging before placing it in the bag. "Bring it with you. We may find something useful downstairs," Elldy suggested.

The two men followed the curator through the museum and down two flights of stairs to the basement area. The space was filled to capacity with shelf upon shelf of artefacts from all corners of the globe.

"The archive room is just through here," Elldy said. She held open the door to what appeared to be a very dingy room filled with books and boxes stacked tightly together in narrow rows. It smelled terribly fusty, and Gredge had a sudden wave of claustrophobia. Feeling panic rising, he backed away from the door.

"I'll stay out here, if you don't mind. I have a slight headache, and I rather think those archives will be of more interest to you than me, Midnight."

"Are you sure, Arthur?" Midnight eyed him with concern.

"Absolutely. I've no desire to look at a bunch of books. I'll just have a look around here," he said, waving a hand vaguely.

"Well, don't touch anything," Elldy stated with a slight air of annoyance. The look on her face suggesting she couldn't understand why anyone with an ounce of sense would not be overjoyed at the prospect of a private tour around her beloved archives.

Gredge nodded in acquiescence, and the curator disappeared with Midnight in tow. Gredge let out a sigh of relief. The thought of being holed up in that stuffy, dark room made him extremely uncomfortable—not that he felt entirely at ease in the almost-windowless basement either.

There were a couple of lit oil lamps dotted around. He took one and began to explore the vast array of exotic artefacts. Most were boxed and labelled, but some of the larger items, such as the gigantic and very fearsome-looking stuffed polar bear, were free standing, and he was able to appreciate them in all their glory at his leisure. He perused the aisles, noting the richly gilded Egyptian sarcophagi, mummified cats, and broken pots until his feet led him to an area darker and dustier than the rest. No shafts of natural light reached this corner of the basement, and the stored objects were covered in a thin layer of grime. Obviously, these had not been part of the main exhibition in some time. Even more obvious was the fact that the museum needed to hire more staff to keep things shipshape.

Ignoring Elldy's specific instruction, Gredge began to poke around in a pile of indeterminable items on a shelf level with his chest. He presumed the bric-a-brac must be props used in themed displays and not the real deal as no great care had been taken to properly store most of them. His fingers brushed against stiff cloth, and he grabbed it, pulling it towards him. He wasn't sure whether it was curiosity or boredom that caused him to untie the leather thong and unwrap the bundle, but he was pleasantly surprised by its contents. The light from the oil lamp caught a glint of silver. As the cloth fell away, the object Gredge held in his hand was revealed.

He placed the oil lamp on the shelf and turned the item over in his hands. It was a mask, carved from wood in the rough shape of a face. He recognised the markings, which were inlaid with silver, as being similar to those on Midnight's cube. He should probably show it to him. It might prove helpful. He traced the silver runes with his index finger. The mask was incredibly light, considering what it was made of, and he wondered what sort of wood it could be. The craftsmanship was spectacular. He might not be particularly interested in history, but he could certainly appreciate the work that had gone into the making of such a piece. The soft light of the lamp continued to flicker and reflect on the silver decoration. It was strangely alluring. He had a sudden and childish urge to put it to his face, thinking to jump out and startle Midnight with it. The moment the mask covered his face, crippling claustrophobia returned.

Gredge dropped the offending object onto the pile of cloth that had bound it, but he could not bring himself to rewrap it. He did not want to handle it again. His head still swimming, he fought off the panic as his brow began to sweat. He could feel his heart rate quicken and his breathing become rapid and shallow. He felt dizzy and disorientated. Grabbing the lamp, the inspector stumbled his way along the aisles, trying desperately to find his way back to the door where Midnight and Elldy were, no doubt, nose-deep in archived papers, oblivious to his struggle. The walls of the basement seemed to close in around him, crushing him, squeezing the breath from his lungs. He had to get out. He needed air. Where were the damned stairs? Gredge lurched sideways into some shelving, causing something to clatter to the floor. The sound hurt his ears. Seconds later, he thought he heard someone call his name, but he couldn't be sure. His hearing was muffled, and his vision was blackening. The last thing he remembered was a touch on his elbow... and then nothing.

"Easy now, Arthur. Don't try to move."

Gredge recognised Midnight's voice as his world came slowly back into focus. His head felt fuzzy, like it was stuffed with cotton rags. Then he became aware of a throbbing pain in his skull. When he touched a tentative hand to his right temple, his fingers came away slippery with blood. The coppery scent made him heave.

"He needs a doctor. Can you manage to get him upstairs? And I'll summon you a cab."

"Yes, thank you, Miss Bird. I can manage him." Midnight shoved a handkerchief in Gredge's hand. "Here. Press this against your head."

Gredge winced but kept the cloth pressed against his wound.

"What happened?" he mumbled.

"You passed out and hit your head," Elldy said. "You need to get this man home," she instructed Midnight.

"Can you stand, Arthur?"

"Think so." Gredge pushed himself to his feet, surprised to find himself on a chair, yet having no memory of getting there.

"You are unsteady. Put your arm around my shoulders and I'll help you upstairs. Miss Bird, would you mind getting the door?"

Between them, they managed to guide Gredge back to the front lobby of the museum, where Elldy left them seated while she went to the entrance to summon a cab.

"You'll feel better soon, Arthur. You'll come back to Meriton where I can take care of you."

"By 'take care of,' you mean jiggery-pokery, right?"

"You can wait for a doctor if you prefer," Midnight stated, a little affronted.

"No offence, but I'm not sure I want—you know…"

"Fine. You'll come to Meriton, and I'll call a doctor."

"It is my bonce, Midnight."

"Indeed, it is."

"I can go home. I'll be fine."

"You may not want me and my *jiggery-pokery* messing around with your *bonce*, as you so eloquently put it, but you are not fine, and you will come to Meriton. You probably have a concussion. Ahh, Miss Bird is back. Up you get."

Arthur had no time to protest before he was hiked up and bundled into the waiting cab outside.

"I wish your friend well, Lord Gunn," Elldy said as she shook Midnight's hand.

"Thank you. I apologise for the disruption."

"No apology needed. I'll be in touch regarding your mysterious cube as soon as I have anything to report."

"I look forward to hearing from you. I appreciate your help. Good day to you, Miss Bird."

"Good day."

Midnight climbed into the cab beside a very green-tinged Gredge. "Meriton House, Berkeley Square," he called to the driver, and the cab lurched forward eliciting a groan from the inspector. "Will you please let me help?" Midnight appealed.

"I'm fine."

"You are stubborn."

"You're pushy," Gredge retaliated and promptly heaved again. Suddenly, the prospect of a comfy bed with fresh sheets and a bit of fuss didn't seem so bad.

2

MERITON HOUSE
DECEMBER 2ND 1862

M idnight was waiting in the corridor outside the
bedroom in which Arthur was now being examined.
He resisted the urge to eavesdrop, granting his friend some
privacy, but he had not liked the look of that head wound at
all. If only Arthur had let him heal him.

The door opened and the doctor exited.

"What's the damage?" Midnight enquired.

"No fracture, you'll be pleased to know. But he does have
a nasty cut and a concussion. I've stitched him up. He should
stay in bed for at least the next twenty-four hours. Any
further vomiting or if he complains of dizziness, send
for me."

"I will. Thank you, Doctor. May I see the patient?"

"You can, but I gave him a draught to help him rest, so
you may find him a little sleepy."

"Fine. Then I will leave him a while. I shall see you out."

"No, no. I can manage. Thank you." Doctor Blanchard
shook Midnight's hand and departed, leaving Midnight to his
thoughts.

It was fortunate that Arthur was asleep, for he had much

on his agenda today. Nurse Carstairs, the woman Midnight had previously employed to care for his housemaid, Laura Carter, and his groom, Charlie Fenwick, during the 'Hemlock incident'—as it was now referred to by the rest of the household—were due at Meriton House to discuss a position at his new charitable hospital, Saint Francis'. There was much to sort out before her imminent arrival. But first, he decided a quick check-in on Polly was overdue before he settled down to his own business. He should really see how her instruction was progressing.

Midnight made his way downstairs to the library, where he found his daughter and her governess, Miss Agnes Carmichael, reciting the eight times table.

"Good afternoon. How is everything today?" he enquired.

"Good afternoon, sir. Miss Polly is doing well, thank you. Although, she does seem a little distracted today," Agnes replied with a slight frown.

"Distracted?" He turned to his daughter, who shrugged.

"I ain't too fond of numbers is all," she explained. "I'm tryin' me 'ardest."

"Darling, do try to remember your elocution," Agnes chided.

"Trying your best is all I expect of—" Midnight stopped midsentence. "Good lord, what is that awful smell?" He sniffed the air.

"Sir?" Agnes looked confused. "I don't smell anything."

"It smells like… wet dog." He eyed his daughter. "Polly, it's coming from you. What on earth have you been up to?"

Polly flashed him an unashamedly innocent look. "Nothin'."

"Hmm." Midnight narrowed his eyes.

"Maybe Laura didn't dry me clothes properly." Polly shrugged.

"I'll see Miss Polly's clothes are sent down to the laundry when she changes for dinner, sir."

"Thank you, Agnes." Then to Polly, Midnight said, "As for you, young lady, see you pay attention to your governess. No more *distractions*." He emphasized the last word.

"Yes, Papa," Polly replied, struggling now to maintain her look of absolute innocence. Midnight gave her a look of disingenuous reproach then turned to address her governess. "Have you had word from home yet?"

"No, sir. I haven't. It's been months since Father's last letter and still no information about my brother. I fear the worst has happened." Agnes swallowed hard and allowed her gaze to drop to the floor.

"Never fear, Agnes. As I've said previously, it is difficult to get mail out of the country at the moment. Once the shipping blockade eases, then I'm sure you'll hear from your brother. Have faith." He fixed her with his best reassuring smile, and she did her best to return it. The American civil war raged on still, and with no immediate end in sight, Midnight secretly suspected that Agnes' concerns were justified. Of course, he would never admit that to her. Why worry the poor woman until worry was her only option?

After leaving the library, Midnight headed back upstairs to Polly's room. Once there, he listened intently, his hand resting on the door handle. Using his extraordinary skills, he probed the atmosphere for any sense of a foreign presence concealed beyond the thick oak door. It didn't take long for him to find one. Pursing his lips, he barged into the room.

"When I agreed to let you stay, I expressly told you that bedrooms were out of bounds." His keen eyes scanned the seemingly empty room and came to rest by the window where the air shimmered ever so slightly. "You are aware that I can see you?"

The shimmer morphed into a ripple that gradually faded away to reveal a giant shaggy canine creature, whose bright eyes twinkled in the light and tongue lolled to out one side of a huge mouth, giving Midnight the impression he was smiling.

"Hello, Widdershins."

The creature chuffed in response.

"You could at least pretend to be remorseful."

Shins, as Polly had affectionately nicknamed him, cocked his head to one side, ears flattened.

"Too late now. I thought we had agreed the stables were to be your guard station during your stay."

Shins growled.

Midnight heard the distant chime of the brass bell at the front door. "We'll discuss this underhanded flouting of the rules later. I have to go. In the meantime, be off with you, and don't scare anyone on your way down. I have visitors this afternoon, so stay out of the way." He stood to the side, holding open the door for the creature to exit.

Shins slinked past him, heckles up, and shot Midnight a look of annoyance before the air around him shimmed again, and the gigantic furry creature disappeared behind his shield of glamour.

On his way downstairs, Midnight found himself wondering, not for the first time, how on earth his life had become so complicated in the time since he had adopted Polly. He craved the days of relative solitude and anonymity that were now long gone.

His household had grown significantly, as had his responsibilities along with his public reputation, the latter not entirely a good thing. It was increasingly difficult to keep what he was under wraps with the ever-more-vigilant and scrutinising eyes of the wider populous into which he was now forced, by his own actions, to expose himself. As Giles continually reminded him, the building and organising of a hospital could not effectively be achieved by taking a back seat, no matter how hard he tried or desired it so. He did not regret the decision to open the facility, but he looked forward to a time in the not-so-distant future when it would be fully up and running, and he could then step back and allow the board of governors to take over. He hankered for those halcyon days when it was him, alone, with just Giles and Mrs P. for company. Then, he immediately regretted such selfish thoughts.

Circumstances had changed dramatically for him, but they had also brought him a daughter in Polly, a friend in Arthur, and an extended household of which he was most fond. Laura's bright smile flashed in his memory, filling him with a warmth tainted by shame. Circumstance was a fickle friend, indeed.

Giles caught Midnight midway down the stairs and informed him that his guest had arrived and was waiting in the front parlour. It was one of those days, of which there were far too many recently, Midnight decided, during which he seemed to jump from one appointment straight to another. He was busy from dawn until dusk, and although it filled his time with meaningful purpose, he did occasionally miss the quiet hours in his study. His night-time wanderings through the rookeries of London had been replaced by bedtime readings of the latest Charles Dickens novel or, Polly's favourite, Grimm's Fairy Tales.

He chuckled to himself, remembering how much his daughter seemed to love the scary parts the most and was always fascinated by the monsters in the stories. Given with whom she lived, it wasn't surprising.

Thinking about his days past made Midnight nostalgic to

be amongst the real people of the city, and he made up his mind to fit in an evening stroll through the darkened streets very soon. For now, he must put on his business head and play at being the perfect gentleman of polite society. It was not a game of which he was overly fond.

3

MERITON

LATER THAT DAY

ℛ‖ℛ

" A pleasure to have you on board, Nurse Carstairs. I will write to you as soon as I have a date for you to commence employment." Midnight took the hand of the broadly smiling woman, and shook it firmly.

"Thank you, Lord Gunn. I am most appreciative of the opportunity. I look forward to working for you," she replied with sincerity.

"Not for me but with me—for the people of London."

"Yes, of course. For the people." Her broad smile was now accompanied by a slight flush of her cheeks. "Pardon me, but I have to say... it is a wonderful thing you are doing, Lord Gunn. Setting up a charity hospital is no mean feat. It is a real honour to be a part of your project." She beamed at him.

Now it was Midnight's turn to feel uncomfortable. Public praise didn't sit well with him. He wasn't at all used to it. Giving an awkward nod in her direction, he rang for his butler. "Giles will see you out. Thank you for coming." He left her in the room, passing Giles on the way out.

Now his business with the nurse was done, he wanted to

check in on his reluctant house guest. "Giles, when you have attended to Nurse Carstairs, would you have Mrs P bring up a tea tray to the inspector's room?"

"Of course, sir." The old butler inclined his head before approaching their visitor to help her into her coat.

Knocking gently on the door to Gredge's room, Midnight waited for a response before entering.

"You're awake, I see."

"Just about," Arthur grumbled.

"I have sent for some tea if you are agreeable to receive company?"

"I suppose I could manage a bite or two."

"Glad to hear it. I'm sure the ever-attentive Mrs Phillips will rustle you up something delightfully delicious, as is her standard."

"Mmm," Gredge replied. The thought of tasty—and free—food gave him a reason for mild cheer at least.

Midnight settled himself into an armchair by the large sash window. "And how are you feeling now you've had a little rest? How's your head?" Midnight asked with genuine concern, for in truth, Arthur still looked decidedly peaky.

"'S'alright, I suppose. I don't know why everyone is fussing. I'm perfectly fine. I'll be off home soon—after I've eaten," Gredge added.

"Absolutely not. You are to stay in bed until tomorrow at the very least. Doctor's orders," Midnight warned as Arthur opened his mouth to protest. "You have suffered a concussion, and I'm to keep an eye on you while you recover. No, Arthur." Midnight held up his hand, effectively shutting down the attempted interruption once again. "The only way you are getting out of this room before morning is if you allow me to heal your injuries. And we both know that is not going to happen, so rest you will and rest you—"

"Will you bloody well let me speak, you infernal know-it-all!" Gredge bellowed, his pasty visage suddenly turning pink with effort.

The room fell silent.

Gredge glared at Midnight, whose lips remained parted, midsentence. "Jesus and Hellfire! You can be so annoying sometimes. You can't control everyone and everything, *Lord Gunn*," Gredge spat. He covered his face with his hands and moaned into them. "I'm perfectly capable of deciding whether or not I am fit enough to go home, thank you very much."

A few painful seconds ticked by where neither man spoke but regarded each other through unfamiliar eyes. Midnight, who, Arthur was sure, was not at all used to being spoken to in such a manner, was utterly speechless for once. A slight frown crossed his brow, and his lips twitched as if he wanted to say something but didn't know what *to* say. And Gredge, who was sweating now with the effort of attempting to rein in his temper, stared at his own balled-up fists.

What was wrong with him? He felt as though there was a pool of volcanic rage in his gut just waiting to erupt. The awkward silence between them hung in the air, thick with volatility, at least on Gredge's part. He felt as though he was the barrel of gunpowder and Midnight the fuse. He knew that, if Midnight spoke, the fuse would be lit, and he would go off like a bomb. Midnight's eyes squinted almost imperceptibly, but Arthur caught it and felt himself inwardly daring the other man to respond.

The unspoken stand-off between them was broken by a knock on the door, and the cheerful tones of Meriton's cook and housekeeper, Mrs Phillips.

When she received no answer, she tried again. "Inspector? I have a tray for you. Can I come in?"

"Yes, do enter," Midnight replied, seeing that Gredge was unable to respond.

The door swung open, and Clementine Philips' voluminous personage bustled into the room. She placed a tea tray, loaded with sandwiches and cake, atop the mahogany occasional table by the window. "Shall I pour?" she asked, turning to face the two gentlemen. Her genial smile faded as she caught a sense of the strained atmosphere in the room.

"Just the one cup. Thank you, Mrs Phillips. I fear I have kept the inspector from his rest for far too long." Midnight rose from the chair at the same time that Arthur swept back the bedcovers and stood up, wobbling slightly, resulting in a shocked squeak from Mrs Phillips, who was looking anywhere but at Scotland Yard's finest who stood brazenly in her presence in nothing but a nightshirt.

"Forgive me, but I am unable to stay for tea. I have pressing police business to attend to. I am leaving." He stressed the last sentence and glared challengingly at Midnight whose expression was unreadable. Reaching for his clothes, which were neatly folded on an ottoman, Gredge steadied himself before declaring, "I should like to get dressed now, if you don't mind."

4

LITTLE SURREY STREET
THE EVENING OF DECEMBER 2ND 1862

ℛ║ℛ

Arthur blotted his latest entry carefully before closing his journal. It was one of several leather-bound volumes he used to jot down his thoughts pertaining to the cases on which he worked through the years. He found documenting the cases both cathartic and useful when he needed to go over a chain of events in the hopes of finding a lead he may have missed.

The chime of the mantle clock struck seven. There was time enough for him to pop down to the Rose and Crown for supper. Patting his stomach, he regretted not staying at Meriton for the inevitable feast that Midnight's cook would have provided. He took in the vista of his compact living room with its worn, comfy armchair by the range, the bare floorboards covered by a substantial, if slightly tatty, rug, the two-seater dining table, and his desk. Never before had a room reflected bachelorhood so candidly as this one.

Donning his signature bowler hat and cocking it slightly so as to hide the bandage then pulling on his trademark long coat, Arthur shoved a few coins in his pocket and set off. The long shadows of twilight coated the pavement on which he walked, causing him to feel chilled. He crossed to the other side of the road, something about the shadows unsettling him. The feeling stayed with him until he reached the corner of the street where the tavern stood. Music and conversation emanated from the building, a welcoming, familiar sound that bathed him with reassurance.

Once he was settled at his favourite seat by the window, the barmaid took his order.

"Steak and kidney, boiled potatoes, and a pint of your best, please, Doris."

"Only got the one ale in today, Inspector. That'll 'ave to do ya."

"As long as it's cold and wet, I'm not fussed."

"It's warm an' watered down. Take it or leave it." Doris grinned.

"Better make it two pints, then, eh?" Arthur countered.

Doris gave him a wink and flounced off.

As he waited, he examined the room, a force of habit for a detective. He took in the same old faces that frequented the tavern almost on a daily basis. Some met his gaze and nodded or raised a glass in acknowledgement, some ignored him, and some slunk discretely out of his view. Most were blissfully unaware of his consideration. These were the people he enjoyed watching the most. Arthur didn't peg himself as much of a conversationalist. He didn't have any particular friends to speak of. Well... Perhaps he would've called Midnight a friend... *Maybe not now,* he thought with a pang of hurt, but he had acquaintances and the camaraderie of the constabulary and that was fine. He was a people watcher. You could say it was a hobby of sorts, one that benefitted his career. You could discover an awful lot about a person's character through discreet observation.

A hearty meal and a few pints later, Arthur left the Rose

and Crown and headed home in the rain. The dull yellow glow of the gaslights barely penetrated the gloomy street. The noise of raucous laughter from the tavern dissipated and the steady pitter-patter of raindrops on roofs became a torrent of water sloshing from the runoff which splashed onto the cobbles, soaking him from head to toe. Arthur shucked up the collar of his coat and set off at a hurried pace, hoping the range at home had remained lit. His irritation at the rain exacerbated when he stepped, ankle deep, in a pothole full of dirty water.

"Damnation!" He hopped out of the puddle almost toppling over on the cobbles. He cringed at the cold squelching in his shoe when he set his foot back on the ground.

By the time he reached home, his mood was as black as the sky. The Gredge residence on Little Surrey Street was a modest middle-terraced one bedroom dwelling. He could've afforded better, but in truth, he had no need of anything larger. It wouldn't do for him to be rattling around in a big house by himself. Having grown up in the area, he was fond of it, warts and all. He had everything he needed, a good job, food in his belly, and a safe place to sleep.

No friends, no wife, no children, said the voice in his head. He ignored it.

Arthur felt the rain trickle down his neck and under his collar. He shivered. Reaching in his pocket, he retrieved the door key. It slipped from his grasp and onto the wet pavement. Things just weren't going his way today. The comfort and warmth of the tavern seemed an age away. There were no street lamps here, so he couldn't see where the key had landed. Arthur grumbled and fumbled around until his hand closed on the cold iron. He plunged the blade of the key into the lock, more forcefully than he'd intended. It was at that particular moment when the skin on the back of his neck prickled.

He paused midturn, his hand still on the key. How was it possible that the street seemed darker than it had just moments ago? He squinted, looking through the rain into the deepest shadows. The street was empty. There were no lights in the windows, but all of his finely tuned senses told him he was being watched.

He resisted the urge to shout, *Go away, Midnight!* because that would invite the meddling swine to make contact with him, and right now, Midnight was the last person he wanted to see. The argument had unsettled him. He was used to the banter between himself and his friend, but this had been wholly different. He had snapped. In all his years in the force, keeping the rookies in line, he had never lost his temper in such a way before.

Arthur closed and locked the door behind him, dropping the key on the little tray atop the hall table. His mind was elsewhere as he removed and hung up his coat and hat. Attempting to self-analyse, he went over the events of the last few months, determined to understand where his sudden aggression had come from. Midnight was right, he hadn't been himself since his return from Scotland. There was no one thing he could think of that could trigger his outburst, however. He had investigated countless cases with Midnight in the past, witnessed an alarming variety of otherworldly creatures, and grown to accept that the unexplainable occurrences he'd been part of were a necessary evil to endure in his particular line of work.

Arthur poured himself a large whisky, tipped it down his throat in one then poured himself another. He wiped a drop from his moustache and gave it a habitual tug. A sense of extreme isolation settled over him, coupled with a level of anxiety that was altogether unfamiliar.

Feeling suddenly reminiscent, he indulged in the urge to read through his older journals. His awareness of being stalked by Midnight in the street had prompted memories from a similar circumstance from when he and Midnight had first encountered each other years ago. Reaching in a drawer, he pulled out a well-worn leather volume and, flicking through to find the relevant entry, began to read about it.

Arrived at the scene at 8:20 p.m. The body was still warm and had the same puncture marks to the neck as the others, although not drained of blood this time. Obviously interrupted the bastard! We're getting closer, though. Got my first look at the swine tonight. Should get the report finished before I retire for the evening. If I can figure out what the hell it was I witnessed.

Lord in Heaven knows how I'm supposed to explain this one to the Guv. Rowe nearly shite himself, poor sod. He's a proper Captain Flashman, that one. Bloody typical P. Division. No balls. Nice boy, though. Keen. Maybe I should have him transferred to me. Make a proper bobby out of him.

I digress. I will try to explain in my own words, the events of this evening, before attempting to write my report.

Me and Rowe rolled up just after dark. We'd been scouting the area after receiving the letter from Y.N. The other two bodies were found by the Victuallers' Asylum in Peckham and on Kent Street near London Bridge. Y.N.'s letter pointed towards the next location being somewhere near Our Lady of Sorrows, down on Friary Road. Turns out it was right on the bleeding' steps of the church. Body laid out as bold as brass but not as neat as the others. This one looked 'unfinished'. That's when we saw it.

I say 'it', because for all it looked like a man, what it did is beyond the realms of human capability. I swear, as I live and breathe, smoke shot out of its hands, like steam from a kettle. Young Rowe actually squealed. I would have laughed had I not been so shocked. The thing was heavily cloaked and was lurking by the corner of the church. Wouldn't have even noticed, had we not startled it. Can't work out why it was hiding in the shadows when it clearly hadn't finished with its victim. I have a mind to think on it as a master artist stepping back to contemplate the composition of a piece. If only we'd gotten there sooner. Could've caught it in the act. Bloody thing buggered off sharpish before Rowe had even picked himself off the floor. Shit.

Gredge half huffed, half chuckled as he continued to flick through the journal and read random snippets. He noticed that more and more entries contained notes about his times with Midnight, and he got to wondering what his life might have been like if the two of them had never met. Would he still be investigating unusual cases? Would he have perhaps taken his career in a different direction, maybe been promoted further by now? Would he have met someone and gotten married, had children even? He closed the journal and shut it away in a drawer.

Well, he thought, *perhaps now is the time to find out.*

5

MERITON
DECEMBER 3RD 1862

ЯⅡR

The study at Meriton House was heavy with silence and shadows, broken only by the intermittent, frustrated sighs of its resident. Midnight's brow furrowed as he sat, deep in thought. He remained oblivious to the darkening of the light around him, and the charged atmosphere, full of concern for his friend.

According to Rowe, the inspector's drinking had increased significantly, not that Midnight had seen much physical evidence of that as yet. After all, supper at the local public house was hardly cause for concern, but the fact that the constable had voiced his concerns did raise alarm bells. The dilemma he faced, however, was what was he to do about it? Should he actually *do* anything at all? Or would the damned stubborn Inspector Gredge not thank him for getting involved and for being a... What had he called him? *An infernal know-it-all?*

A low growl startled him from his reverie. Two glowing eyes emerged from the inky darkness that had now engulfed the room. Widdershins stalked cautiously towards the desk where Midnight stiffened, suddenly on guard, noticing the raised heckles on the creature's neck.

"What is it?" Midnight hissed, eyes travelling quickly from corner to corner, attempting to locate the danger whilst also wondering why his own senses had failed to pick up any threat.

Shins whined a little then chuffed at Midnight, dipping his heavy head at the deepening shadows. It was then that Midnight understood the reason why his senses had supposedly failed him.

"My apologies. I had not realised," he said, abashed. It had been a while since he had lost his grasp on the shadows. His concern for Gredge had clearly penetrated his control.

Midnight closed his eyes briefly and inhaled slow and deep. As he did so, the shadows receded, and the room morphed back into its usual, pleasant, organised state.

The barghest's heckles flattened, and the tension melted away from its bulky frame. Shins sneezed derisively and fixed Midnight with a look of reprimand.

"I said I was sorry. What more do you require? And besides, this is my house, in case you are unaware. I will not be chastised by a *dog.*"

Shins bared his teeth.

"Fine! By a *mutt.*" Midnight shrugged one shoulder at Shins, to which the creature promptly turned its back on him and started towards the exit. "Wait!" Midnight cried, a sudden idea entering his head. "I need you to do something for me."

Shins stopped, one paw in the air as if deciding whether or not to stay and listen.

"Gredge is in trouble, and I think you can help him."

Shins pricked up his ears.

"Please?" Midnight implored. "He is my friend... I will let you sleep in Polly's room tonight."

The mutt's haunches jiggled, and he turned his head to look Midnight in the eye.

Incredulous, Midnight continued. "Are you... *laughing?* Why you deplorable—"

Shins chuffed again and padded back in to the study to sit, upright and attentive, by the fire.

"I should think so, too," Midnight scolded. "Our inspector is not well, as you may know. It is my belief that something untoward may have happened to him up on the hill that night by the standing stones. When I was down on the ground and the portal opened, I saw someone... or something attempting to break through." He paused, trying to think how best to word his request. "Is it possible that something *did,* and that it has somehow affected Arthur? Would you enter the... *otherworld* and see what you can find out?"

The creature shook his head.

"Why not?" Midnight asked.

Shins blew air out heavily from his nostrils.

"I do not know what that means. Oh, this is ridiculous. I am attempting to have a meaningful conversation with an animal. It is never going to work." He ran his palm over his face, sighing. "If you would just let me see for myself—"

Shins growled, flattening his ears.

"Fine! I won't touch you although that seems to me to be the quickest way to understand what you are saying."

Shins chuffed again and pointed his nose at the ceiling.

"What now? I do not understand what you are telling me!"

He could have sworn the mutt rolled his eyes in exasperation before he looked up at the ceiling again and barked. Realisation hit.

"Ah, of course. You want to fetch Polly."

Shins wagged his tail and rambled quickly from the room

in search of the girl. She and the creature had a special connection; they were able to communicate telepathically somehow, a trick that caused the pair of them to get into a lot of trouble of late, and one that Midnight wished he possessed.

It was damned inconvenient that the dog would not allow him inside his head. Since that night on the hill, Shins had communicated to Polly that Midnight's touch disturbed his equilibrium, to which Polly had said that she didn't know what that meant and so had just told her father that he made Shins feel all 'squiffy'. However, on an occasion such as this, being able to directly 'talk' to the animal would've proven most useful.

Midnight poured himself a large tumble full of his favourite libation—twelve-year-old French brandy—while he waited for them to return. Taking a large sip, he welcomed the heat of the liquid as it travelled pleasingly down his throat, temporarily quelling his concerns.

Whatever had appeared inside the portal that night must have something to do with the inspector's troubles. Of course it must. He was only human. He had no special powers, like Midnight, or extra-sensory abilities as did Polly. There was nothing to protect Arthur from otherworldly influences, and he had been exposed to many since making Midnight's acquaintance.

Sudden crushing guilt lay like a stone blanket around his shoulders. This was his fault. He had underestimated the effects his dealings with the good inspector would have. He had taken Arthur's participation in, and acceptance of, his world for granted. The question he now faced was: What should he do about it?

6

STONES END

JANUARY 8TH 1863

ℛℛ

"Years of loyal service, and that's it? Suspended without pay? Am I hearing you right?" Gredge bellowed.

"Am I hearing you right, *Superintendent*," Robert Branford corrected him. "Sit down, Gredge."

"*Inspector* Gredge," Arthur countered, which his super parried.

"That remains to be seen."

Twenty years Gredge's senior, Superintendent Branford was someone of notoriety within the London Metropolitan Police, and deeply respected by his colleagues and his community. Despite the relatively small size of his office at Stones End—M. Division's headquarters—Brandford's presence dominated the cramped space like a king in his palace, the well-worn leather of the captain's chair his throne. He commanded respect without ever raising his voice, and Gredge immediately regretted his outburst.

He cleared his throat, tugged his moustache, and took a seat as instructed, trying his damnedest to appear outwardly calm even though his emotions were raging.

Branford raised his dark head from the papers he was

signing to pin his subordinate with an appraising look, the briefest hint of concern behind his deep brown eyes. "You have changed," he stated. "A year ago, you would not have spoken to a superior officer like that."

"Why does everyone keep saying that? I haven't changed at all. I'm exactly the same as I've always been. I'm just annoyed at this bloody shambles. You know me, sir. And you know I do not deserve to be punished because some drunk-arsed woman thinks every man in a mac and bowler is a child killer!" Gredge realised his voice had risen an octave again. He blew out a heavy, sharp breath of frustration from between tightened lips and looked at the ceiling, shaking his head in disbelief.

"You seem very angry, Gredge. And before you interrupt me again, I mean of late, not just this moment. In all the years I have known you and had the honour of working with you, I have never known you to miss a day of work or arrive late... until these last few months. You cannot account for your whereabouts on the estimated time of the murders. Indeed, you cannot even remember what day it is lately. Do I believe you are a killer? I would like to say no, probably not. Am I concerned about your recent conduct? Yes, very much so, and because of this, I must insist you take some time away. A... sabbatical, if you like."

"Sabba—! Oh, Hell's teeth. Just call it what it is, will you? It's a bloody suspension. You're taking my badge and my gun, for Christ's sake!" Gredge raged, incredulous.

"You know that, and I know that, but no one else has to. However, I do feel that, due to your..." Branford paused, searching for the correct term, "...*instability* at the moment, you are a threat to yourself and the integrity of this office of investigation. And I certainly cannot have you anywhere near this case until we can positively put you in the clear. You must see that."

Gredge pursed his lips, making his moustache twitch. He matched the super's stare with his own squinty appraisal and then said, "This is bloody Labalmondiere, isn't it? He's never liked me. I know damned well this hasn't come from you."

Branford sighed.

"What the commissioner may or may not have said is not your concern right now. Your concern should be for yourself —as is mine for you. Arthur, you are a good officer and an honourable man, from what I have seen. Take the time out, and let us do our jobs. Take a walk in the park, rest, and get your head straight. Just... make sure to stay in the city. Alright?"

Gredge stood and loosened his pistol from its holster. He placed it firmly on Branford's desk along with his identification badge. He ran his tongue along the front of his teeth and smacked his lips loudly before striding to the door. He had planned on giving it a good old slam in his wake but was surprised to see Rowe waiting outside the door in the corridor.

His junior's look of concern made him chuckle sardonically. "Smile, Rowe. You're about to get a promotion." Gredge patted Rowe's shoulder as he turned and stalked away.

The last thing Gredge heard as he reached the end of the corridor was Branford's deep dulcet tones. "Come in, Constable Rowe."

Gredge was seething. Anger and betrayal flowed through his veins like liquid fire. Ignoring the hails and salutations from his colleagues, he stormed out of the heavy studded oak door of Stones End police station and out into the cold drizzle of the January morning.

The snow on the ground had receded a little since yesterday, and the smattering of rain and freezing temperatures had turned it crunchy and slick underfoot. Arthur skidded on the stone steps that lead from the entrance to the cobbled street below, nearly losing his balance. He managed to save himself from falling by grabbing on to the thick iron railing of the steps. The icy cold metal burned his hand.

"Bollocks!" he shouted into the slight wind that now accompanied the freezing rain, the truly miserable day mirroring his emotions.

Steadying himself, Arthur adjusted the collar of his coat to shield his ears from the biting weather, stuffed his gloveless hands into his pockets, and made his way down the street, allowing the hustle and bustle of the heavily peopled morning to swallow him up.

Just as the dull dampness of the London smog threatened to erase his hunched silhouette, another taller, slimmer figure emerged from the shadows, encapsulated within the folds of a heavy coat, tweed cap pulled low to hide his face. The figure stared for a moment in the direction the inspector had gone then followed him into the gloom.

7

MERITON

DECEMBER 24TH 1862

Я|R

" 'Twas the night before Christmas
When, all through the house,
Not a creature was stirring, not even a mouse.
The stockings were hung by the chimney with care
In hopes that St. Nicholas soon would be there."

Miss Carmichael paused, waiting for her charge to continue the rhyme. It was one they had been practicing in readiness for Miss Polly's performance later that evening after dinner. However, the child was not paying attention. Polly's gaze was directed towards the door that led from the parlour, in which she and her governess were seated by the fire.

"I do not think he will come, dear one," Miss Carmichael said, her American accent soft with sympathy.

"He has to, Aggie. He wouldn't let us down." Her gleaming eyes betrayed the uncertainty of her declaration.

Agnes closed the little red book of children's rhymes she had been reciting from and reached for Polly's hand. "Darling, your papa has not heard from the inspector since the day he left Meriton. I highly doubt he will come this evening. Please, do not get your hopes up. Besides," she said cheerily, "you will still have an attentive audience to entertain. Now, are we going to practice one last time?"

"Nah. I know it off by 'eart, Aggie." The little girl shrugged looking downhearted. Polly blew out a frustrated sigh and fiddled with the ribbon on her sleeve.

"Very well. We still have a few hours before dinner. Shall we finish making the decorations?" The governess rose, retrieved a basket full of crafting materials from an occasional table and jiggled it tantalisingly at Polly. "Let us make our tree the best-decorated tree in the city. What do you say?" Agnes wiggled her eyebrows and grinned.

Polly couldn't resist an opportunity to get thoroughly messy with glue and paper and so nodded her head vigorously in agreement.

They had barely begun when the sound of a bell rang clear and loud from the street. Soon after, a choir of voices in song drifted mutedly into the parlour.

Miss Carmichael went to the window and exclaimed, "Carollers! How delightful. We rarely get those in New York. Get your shawl, Miss Polly, then run to the kitchen and tell Mrs Phillips and the others, will you? I will fetch your father. Hurry now."

Polly grabbed her woollen shawl and sprinted through the house to the kitchen. When she excitedly burst through the door—yelling, "Mrs Phillips! Laura! Charlie! Come quickly. They're singing!" —a tsunami of deliciousness drowned her senses. Polly stopped in her tracks and inhaled deeply. Her eyes closing in sheer ecstasy with the smells of freshly baked pies, cinnamon, sugar biscuits, and mulled cider. "'Cor!" She drooled.

Mrs Phillips started at the interruption. "Goodness!

What's this now, miss? There's no point in trying to charm a treat out of me before dinner. Off with you now, and let me get on." She flapped a floured tea cloth at the young girl, sending a flurry of white motes into the warmed air that floated gently to the floor like snow.

"Aggie sent me to fetch you. There's singers outside!" she squealed excitedly, her curls bouncing.

"Singers? Well, then. Come on. Give me a hand with these pies."

Polly scooted forward to grab a tray full of steaming hot mince pies from the rotund cook.

"Can you manage?" Mrs Phillips asked her, knowing the large tray may be too much for the girl with her missing left hand.

She needn't have asked, though, as Polly grinned and rested the tray on the scarred stump of her left arm, gripping the tray tightly with her right hand. The offending hand had been amputated due to the damage caused by years of poisoning from selling matches on the streets of the city. Yet this bright little bean never let her disability hold her back from doing anything.

"Off we go then." Mrs Phillips chivvied Polly along whilst Laura and Charlie gladly abandoned their tasks to follow. Summoning Giles Morgan, the household butler, from his little sitting room with a passing knock on the door— "Carollers, Mr Morgan!"—Mrs Phillips carried on without stopping for an answer.

Miss Carmichael was waiting at the door, but there was no sign of the master of the house. She approached the cook and Polly as they neared.

"Has Lord Gunn gone out? I cannot find him in the library nor his study."

"Allow me, miss," Giles offered as he appeared in the

hallway doing up the buttons of his tailcoat. Giles smiled at the quintet of excited faces by the door and disappeared through another that lead to the library. Miss Carmichael frowned and opened her mouth as if she were about to speak but was interrupted by Polly tugging impatiently on her skirts.

"Papa will be here soon. Can we open the door, pleeease?" she begged. "We're going to miss it."

"And these pies are growing cold," Mrs Phillips added helpfully.

They opened the front door to a most joyous scene. Berkeley Square was awash with golden light emanating from the myriad of lanterns that surrounded the group of carollers, who were belting out the chorus of 'Good King Wenceslas' in perfect harmony. Other residents in the square had emerged from their homes to welcome the singers with offerings of coin for their charity collection box, hot mulled cider, sugar biscuits, and Mrs P's gloriously plump—and very potent—pies. Delicate snowflakes softly kissed the icy ground, settling on trees and twigs as they fell from the clouded sky, dancing and twirling in the warm glow of the lanterns.

"Ooo!" exclaimed Polly, eyes bright with wonder.

A chestnut seller had pitched his cart nearby, and a queue was already forming with people eager to purchase the freshly roasted treats. Neighbours greeted each other and exchanged season's salutations. Happy chattering and bursts of laughter mingled with the harmonious vocals of the choir.

"Happy birthday, sweetheart."

"Papa!" Polly whirled around to find her father standing behind her on the steps of Meriton House, clad in his best dinner jacket and woollen overcoat.

Mrs Phillips smiled and offered him the tray of pies, from

which he took one graciously. Laura and Charlie had joined the line for the chestnuts, and Giles was taking in the scene, a look of happy nostalgia on his aged face. Polly thought her heart might burst with joy as she slipped her little hand into her father's big one. The only thing that would make this night perfect was the presence of dear Inspector Gredge.

Such a merry scene it was that, when Polly glanced up at her father, she was startled to see him staring across the square into an unlit corner, tight lipped and frowning. Following the direction of his gaze, she squinted into the shadows but could not see whatever it was that had caught her father's attention. She concentrated harder on his person.

"Papa? What's wrong? Your colours are all dark."

Knowing that he could not ignore her knack for reading auras, or 'colours' as she liked to call them, he was forced to answer her. "I am not sure, little one. The shadows were bothering me for a moment." He gave her shoulder a reassuring squeeze. "It is likely nothing, just me being overprotective again." Midnight looked down at her and winked, noting that the concern did not leave her. "Ahh! Here is your Miss Carter back with more treats!" That worked.

Laura Carter, Meriton's housemaid and Polly's favourite champion since she had belted someone 'right in the mush', as Polly had told it, approached the small gathering with a beaming smile and offered the little miss a dip in the treat bag.

"Mind your fingers, now, miss. They're hot." The young woman and Charlie offered up their bags of delicious Christmas fare to each of their colleagues in turn.

"Sir?" Laura shyly enquired of her master. "Would you like one?"

"Thank you, Miss Carter. Very kind," Midnight replied, managing to keep from looking directly at his employee.

Polly scrunched up her nose in unabashed disappointment at the stilted exchange between her two favourite people. She had been so excited to visit Scotland, and was keen to see the rebuild and refurbishment of the castle her father had purchased for them as a summer retreat, but she could not help her frustration at the monumental—at least in her eyes—and decidedly unwelcome changes in behaviour the trip had wrought upon those she held most dear—including the inspector, of whom she had grown quite fond.

How taxing being a grown up must be. They seemed to her to always be harried and in a mad rush hither and dither, worrying about all manner of unimportant things. Like laundry and rules. There were no such concerns in her previous life as an orphan. She had sold matches on the streets of London in order to buy herself a bit of stale bread or leftovers from the costermonger's cart at the end of the day's trading. And if she were lucky and earned enough, she might afford a bed for the night by the hearth of the dockyard bawdy house. In a moment of nostalgia, Polly recalled the blissful relief of a night by the warm fire in the company of Madame Le Blanc's ladies. On the odd occasions that she could afford it, a kindly, motherly woman named Sophia would make her up a bed from old blankets and feed her a hot bowl of soup. Which was especially welcome on the harsh winter evenings, when sleeping rough in the doorways of shops and warehouses posed the question as to whether or not she would wake up at all the next morning. Many of her old pals had perished that way. Polly gave an involuntary shiver.

"Are you cold, Miss Peeps?" Midnight asked, using the nickname he had assigned to her on account of her unbound curiosity and penchant for peeping around corners to 'observe' people without their knowledge. He adjusted the shawl that hung loosely around her shoulders to cover her more effectively. "Perhaps we should go inside now? I'm sure Mrs Phillips will be keen to get on with the dinner."

The staff took their cue and turned back towards the house, Polly being the only one to protest at having to leave the frivolity in the square.

"Five more minutes, please, Papa?" she pleaded, giving him her best smile but to no avail.

Midnight guided her towards the entrance, and they stepped inside. He gave the square a final once-over and shut the door. Something was decidedly off about him this evening, Polly decided, and she didn't like it, not one bit.

JOURNAL ENTRY OF D.I. ARTHUR GREDGE

DECEMBER 24, 1862

W*hat is wrong with me?*

I went to Meriton this evening full of contrition and with the intention of fulfilling my promise to Miss Polly to attend her birthday dinner. When I arrived in the square, it was full of people revelling in the spirit of the season, and I became so inexplicably angry! So much so that I could not for the life of me force myself to take another step. I hid in the darkness like some malevolent, envious creature.

He saw me. I know he did. And I wanted to rip out his eyes.

Where has this sudden and uncontrollable rage come from?

The last thing I recall is his piercing stare as he spotted me hunkered against a wall like some snivelling rat. It is clear now that I am no longer welcome at Meriton House. Should I have made my presence known at his door, he would surely have turned me away.

I am home now and writing this entry as I cannot remember how I arrived here. One moment, I was ankle deep in snow and gutter mulch in Berkeley Square, the singing grating heavily on my nerves, and the next, I was here.

I fear I am losing my mind.

Gredge placed his pen back in the ink pot and blotted his words before closing the volume. He ran a hand over his face. Weary and confused, he made his way upstairs to his bedroom. Passing the rack of coat hooks, he failed to notice his filthy mac that hung there and the dripping water that had formed a little puddle on the floor underneath. Nor did he see the delicate lace handkerchief with the initials A.P. embroidered in neat gold stitches poking out provocatively from the pocket, the letter P overlain and stained by a smear of dried, dark red blood.

8

CHURCHYARD
DECEMBER 5TH 1862

The winter sky fell on them like a blanket of ice, and there was no light in the graveyard from which to draw upon to warm himself. Midnight shot Shins an envious look as the creature shook his thick fur tauntingly. Midnight shivered, his breath billowing from chilled lips in long, steaming clouds. How glad he was for the woollen coat and leather gloves, at least. The dark silhouette of the little church was barely visible against the whispering skeletons of the trees with no moon to highlight it. The churchyard was empty save for them, the dead, and their secrets.

"Well?" Midnight urged his uneasy companion, who was doing his best to ignore him.

Shins surveyed their surroundings surreptitiously before padding out from his hiding place behind a large stone memorial. As he neared the building, he glanced back towards where Midnight stood, shrouded in the natural shadows of the night.

Shins had warned Midnight that under no circumstances must he use his powers while the portal was open, lest he attract the attention of whatever malevolence might be lurking on the other side. Polly, who had negotiated the terms of this little escapade between him and the animal, had, of course, wanted to come along but had been issued a firm no by both Midnight and Shins. On that, at the very least, they had agreed. The downside of this was that he could not fully communicate with Shins without her.

The mutt agreed to let Midnight company him as far as the church but no further; declaring the Otherworld as unsafe for one such as himself. In truth, Midnight was most curious about the 'Other' after having been captivated by the tantalising glimpse of what lay beyond his own reality that night upon the hill amongst the ancient stones.

"Make haste, Widdershins," Midnight urged, keen to witness the event.

He watched with increasing interest as the creature set off at a fair pace, running anti-clockwise around the little church. Upon the third pass, Midnight felt the change in the atmosphere, the barely noticeable vibrations underfoot, the way the evening now held the tang of something earthy, like the breeze after the rain has stopped. He focused on the weathered Celtic cross monument by the church where Shins had communicated that the way would open. He expected to see the same, intense blue light that had manifested on that Scottish hilltop, but it was not so.

There was merely a shimmer, a rippling of the air around the stone cross before a circular hole appeared in the landscape. A dim glow emanated from inside it briefly, casting the silhouette of Widdershins in a subtle ethereal light. Shins gave one backward glance then stepped through onto the ley line that would traverse him across the country to his destination. Exactly where that was, the mutt would not reveal. Midnight had questioned him many times, but he had not gotten much satisfaction.

Polly had once said, "Shins says that the Other ain't for the likes of us to be knowing about and that the very fact we know anything at all is dangerous. So, he'll thank you to stop askin' about it. Oh, and he also says the roast lamb smells delightful and would you ask Mrs Phillips for the bone?"

Midnight strained to see what lay beyond, keen to get a closer look. Perhaps if he just crept forward...

The portal was rippling again. Shins was all the way in now, and the opening began to fade. Midnight hurried forward, stumbling on a fallen gravestone in his bid to see. He uttered an involuntary grunt, and Shins snapped his head around in time to see Midnight topple to the ground. He barked once in reproach and failed to see the horde of dark, misshapen beings that were about to fall upon him.

"Look out!" Midnight cried, struggling to his knees.

Too late. The creatures snatched at the Barghest, snagging his fur with clawed hands and beating him with spiked clubs. His lupine form was overwhelmed, despite his bulk and gnashing teeth, and Shins was dragged away. The portal was almost shut, a few more seconds and Midnight would be able to do nothing to help.

He drew deeply on the eager shadows, and they rushed to him, soaking through his skin and filling every part of his body with a familiar pain—a pain that he now relished since he had learned to control both shadow and light. Directing his aim towards the shrinking portal, Midnight fired a billowing trail of his dark power at it. His ammunition penetrated the veil, and his aim was true. The black smoke struck one of the attacking creatures, and it disintegrated into a pile of ash and embers.

Shocked in to momentary inaction, Midnight stared in disbelief. "Well, that was new."

The portal closed. Shins was gone. And Midnight was left

alone in the graveyard to ponder what sort of magic he had produced and how.

He had never made anything explode with his power before. Was this new development something to do with being close to this particular portal? Nothing like that had happened at the stones in Scotland. Or could it be that his abilities were changing as he aged? The latter was the most likely answer, he thought. His abilities had not mutated in a long while. He did not count the moment when he had learned to blend both dark and light when he'd fought Hemlock on Westminster Bridge whilst rescuing his daughter. His powers had not changed then; they had simply blended, allowing him full control. What had happened just now though, that was decidedly different and somewhat alarming.

9

MERITON

JANUARY 11TH 1863

The bell in the basement room tinkled twice, indicating that something urgent was in need of attention. Giles knew that when Midnight was locked away in his secret lair, he was not to be disturbed unless it was absolutely necessary. Bad things could happen if distraction got in the way of his alchemical or supernatural practices. When the bell interrupted his studies, Midnight immediately put aside his work and made his way back up the stone steps that led to the small antechamber attached to the grand library, which functioned as his study. Pulling the rope that caused the false bookshelf to swivel outwards, Midnight found Giles already waiting for him.

"Giles. What is it?"

"You have a visitor. Sergeant Rowe is waiting in the front parlour, and he has news of the inspector."

"*Sergeant?*" Midnight said, surprised.

"Apparently so." Giles shrugged one shoulder.

They found Rowe nervously pacing the length of the Persian rug, but he was not dressed in his usual police uniform.

"Good evening," Midnight said. "Am I correct in assuming that congratulations are in order?"

Rowe turned swiftly at the greeting. "Eh?"

"Mr Morgan, here, informs me that you are now a sergeant?"

"Oh. Yeah. Thank you, but that's not why I'm 'ere."

"Indeed. Mr Morgan has informed me of that also." Midnight gave a placatory smile. "So, then, what news have you of Inspector Gredge?" He indicated for Rowe to sit down before taking his own seat. "Brandy?"

"No, thanks." Rowe waved the offer away. "Don't think I'll ever drink again after what I've seen lately." He sighed, and Midnight waited patiently for him to carry on. "It's the inspector, you see; he's been drinking his days away since his suspension."

Midnight sat forward in his seat.

"Gredge has been suspended?"

Rowe nodded. "You didn't know?"

"No. He hasn't seen fit to inform me of that," Midnight stated sadly. "I have not seen him in quite some time."

"Oh."

"We are not exactly on speaking terms at the moment."

"Oh," Rowe said again, shifting in his seat. "Maybe I should go, then?" He began to rise.

"No. Please, sit. We may not be friendly right now, but Gredge is still my friend. If something is wrong, then I would like to know."

"Well…" Rowe chewed his lip. "It's just that I wanted to come to you first, see, 'cause I found this handkerchief, and I know I should take it to the chief and all, but I just can't get me 'ead around why it would've been in the boss' pocket and… and…" Rowe was rambling at speed now, and Midnight could make no sense of what the trouble was.

"Sergeant Rowe, why don't you take a deep breath and start from the beginning? Let's start with why Gredge has been suspended, shall we?"

Rowe took an exaggerated inhalation and then blurted out, "He's under suspicion for murder."

A heavy and sudden silence descended on the room, the atmosphere thick with disbelief and a thousand unanswered questions. Midnight found he could not speak. He was questioning whether or not he had heard the man correctly. Arthur Gredge, a *murderer?*

"This is clearly a mistake." He had meant it to sound like a statement of fact but could not help the slight hint of doubt from creeping into his words. He thought back to past months as he'd watched his friend's countenance change. He recalled how Gredge's behaviour had been oddly troubling of late, and then he considered Shins, who had gone into the Other to investigate if Gredge could somehow have been affected by a spirit or possession.

Like Hemlock Nightingale, he thought.

"Exactly what I thought too. I mean he ain't been himself lately. That's true enough. But I would've staked my pension on him not being a killer. That is… until today."

Midnight frowned as he watched Rowe reach into his pocket and pull out a dainty piece of white cloth before laying it out on the chair arm.

"Amelia Prescott, a governess at Kingsley House on Berkeley Square, went missing on Christmas Eve as she was walking home to her parents' residence in Cadogen Square Gardens. She was due to spend the night with them to celebrate Christmas the next day. We found her body on December twenty-sixth in Green Park, all peaceful and laid on her side on a park bench. Just looked like she was sleeping or that she'd passed out, maybe had one too many tipples.

The inspector wasn't convinced she'd died from exposure or some other natural cause. He said she looked too perfect, almost like the body had been arranged that way." He paused and asked for a glass of water. Giles quickly obliged.

Midnight's heart had skipped a beat at the mention of Berkeley Square. He recalled his feeling of unease and the sense of Arthur's presence hidden in the shadows near Kingsley House on the very night of December twenty-fourth.

"And what has this—" Midnight indicated the square piece of silk. "—got to do with the unfortunate Miss Prescott and the inspector?"

Rowe picked it up and handed it to Midnight.

"There's the initials A.P on it, see? And... blood. Now, why would he have that in his pocket, eh? It was never documented amongst the evidence at the scene; no mention of any silk handkerchief in the report."

"As you say, he has been acting a tad strangely of late, forgetful even. Perhaps he found it at the scene and put it in his pocket and merely forgot about it? It is entirely possible. Quite honestly, I don't see how such a mistake is enough to tar and feather the man." Midnight regarded Rowe speculatively. "Unless... there's something else?"

"Two more bodies turned up at the docks on Tuesday. Kids. A boy and a girl. Same sort of thing; no obvious cause of death and both laid out side by side like they were sleeping. There were a couple of witnesses who knew the kids. Said they'd seen 'em knocking around the day before, offering to polish shoes for coin. It was me that interviewed 'em, see? And... well, I asked 'em if they'd seen anyone who seemed especially interested in the little 'uns, and they said yes. I was taking down the details when the two women became upset. One of 'em kept sayin', 'It's him, it's him!

He's the fella.' And well…" He paused, not being able to say what he needed to say.

The skin prickled on the back of Midnight's neck. "They identified Gredge?" he said, incredulously.

"There's more."

Midnight could tell that Rowe was struggling now. The young sergeant was hunched forward in the chair, his arms resting on his knees whilst he wrung the tweed cap he was holding between his hands. Midnight waited for Rowe to deliver more revelations regarding his friend and colleague.

"The day the inspector got suspended, the superintendent hauled me into his office and told me to keep watch on him, like. I was to follow him, day and night, and see where he went, who he met, and what he got up to. I didn't want to at first. It don't feel right, spying on the boss. But Branford— he's the super—he said if I wanted to help the inspector, then I shouldn't feel bad 'cause I'd just be doing my job."

Perceptive as ever, Midnight took advantage of the break in Rowe's tale to reply.

"And since you are now here, in my home, telling me all of this, I'm assuming you have observed our dear Gredge doing something he shouldn't be?"

"Yes. He keeps going back to the scenes of the crimes. I mean, it's all very strange. He's not even hiding it, doing it in broad daylight most times. I mean, it perhaps doesn't sound too strange. I suppose he could just have decided to carry on with the investigation despite his suspension. But when he gets to the location, he doesn't do anything. Just stands and stares." Rowe's voice climbed an octave as he continued to explain his concerns.

It was clear to Midnight that the young man was battling with loyalty to Gredge and his loyalty to the Yard, but he still could not yet understand what Rowe hoped to achieve by coming to him first. At best, all this evidence was circumstantial, and very likely, Arthur would have a good explanation for it, wouldn't he?

"I see. And what is it you want me to do to help?"

"Well... I know I ain't supposed to talk about you know... your *abilities* and all," Rowe stammered, "but it's just that I notice things, and you and I, we've worked together with the inspector for a while now so... I just wondered, if I could get you into the mortuary—"

"You want me to look at the bodies?"

"Yes. If you would. You've done it before on cases, and well, I dunno exactly what it is you do, but could you do it now? For the inspector, like? Perhaps whatever you discover, it might help get him off the hook."

Rowe looked so pleadingly at him that Midnight had no trouble agreeing to his request. In fact, now that the sergeant had explained what had been going on these last weeks with his boss, it seemed like the only logical thing to do at this moment. Depending on the time that had elapsed between now and the time of death, he should still be able to view those last critical moments of each victim's life by tapping into their memories, ergo putting Gredge in the clear.

"When would you be able to do it?" Rowe asked.

"No time like the present. That is, if you aren't already committed this evening and the access to the bodies isn't too restricted."

"No, I am not busy at present. All three victims are being stored at the new house for the dead in Westminster. We'll go now, then, eh? It's past seven now. By the time we get down there, it'll be nearly a quarter to eight. Place should be empty by then—no gawkers, at least, just the night attendant. How much time will you need?" said Rowe.

"It all depends on the condition of the remains and how

much time has elapsed since their deaths. Memories fade as the body decomposes, but I shall do what I can," Midnight assured the young copper.

"Thank you, Lord Gunn. I do hate to put you to any trouble, but you're the only one I can think of who might help the inspector. I don't think he's a killer any more than you are."

If only you knew, Midnight thought as memories of the two victims he'd left behind at The Rainbow Club flashed in his mind. Nevertheless, he smiled graciously at Rowe, accepting the backhanded compliment.

They took a Hansom cab rather than Gunn's personal carriage as it was faster and less conspicuous. When one was planning an evening raid on the mortuary, it paid to be discreet.

Midnight and Rowe alighted from the cab just past the new Westminster Bridge a little way from the main building of St. Thomas' Hospital. Midnight glanced back into the murky waters of the Thames where the deadly currents swirled beneath the stone arches.

He still could not pass by this spot without thinking of that frightening night with Polly and Gredge—who had been held to ransom in those freezing waters—and the subsequent fight with Hemlock Nightingale, the human-demon hybrid that plagued his dreams still. He wondered what had become of his enemy's corpse, last seen still, defeated, and presumed dead atop a hill in Scotland.

Since Gredge's discovery that the body had disappeared, both he and the inspector had found themselves once again looking over their shoulders, wondering who or what had taken Hemlock's mutilated remains and why.

They had been through so much together, he and Arthur. A wave of guilt hit him in the chest, bringing him back to the present and the grim task ahead.

"Lead the way, Sergeant." Midnight indicated to the young officer.

The street by the hospital was well lit; the gas lamps glowed, casting their flickering light across the cobbles. At this very moment, Midnight felt as though all the lime lights of the London theatres were upon him, announcing to all who passed by that he was here and planning something dastardly. He followed Rowe down the side of the main building towards a shadowy corner at the rear. Midnight's relief at the shelter the near darkness offered was clear. Attempting to reanimate the dead was not something one should perform under a spotlight.

10

ST. THOMAS'
JANUARY 11TH 1863

Dealing with the night attendant proved easier than they anticipated; the fool of a man had fallen asleep on duty. He hardly flinched when Rowe broke open the lock and he and Gunn crept into the dimly lit hallway of the building. The overweight fellow was slumped in his chair, snoring blissfully. His ample body spilled over the trouser belt at his waist and jiggled with each snort from the man's open mouth. Rowe approached him, his own wooden truncheon raised, and clobbered the man on the side of his head just hard enough to make sure he remained unconscious for a while.

"There. That should keep him out of our hair, give you enough time to 'ave a proper look."

Midnight raised an eyebrow at the young sergeant, who shrugged one-shouldered back at him.

The two men continued on, exploring the various corridors and reading the engraved plaques on each of the doors until they found the one they were looking for.

"The woman will be in here, the kids in a different room." According to Rowe, cadavers were stored in various ways, depending on the particular class and social standing of the victim. Even more macabre, Rowe revealed that the people of the city had developed a new pastime in recent months; the dead were sometimes placed in the waiting morgue. This was the area where the newly deceased were put on display for public view. The waiting morgue served a dual purpose; it satisfied the gawking public's innate sense of morbid curiosity but also gave the corpse a reasonable amount of time to wake up. This was a relatively new practice, Rowe informed him, due to the fact that too many people were being buried alive.

Having located the body of Miss Amelia Prescott, Rowe drew back the sheet of white linen to reveal a face that was on the verge of the later stages of putrefaction. The once delicate features looked swollen, and her skin held a distinct tinge of green with swatches of red, indicating that her blood had begun to decompose. The raised hump beneath the linen cloth barely disguised the bloated stomach, full of the gases caused by the decomposition process. There was evidence of some attempt at a post-mortem as a few stitches were visible near her décolletage.

"I am not sure how much can be determined from this woman's body," Midnight admitted. "She may be way beyond my reach now. But I will try," he added, seeing clear disappointment on the young sergeant's face. "Would you mind leaving the room? I prefer to work in privacy, and it would also serve to keep a look out for the attendant, should he waken." Midnight knew there was no chance of the latter in truth, but it served him well to not have Rowe witness what he was about to do. Even a hardened detective, such as Gredge, had trouble accepting Midnight's darker abilities. Rowe would very likely soil himself.

Once Rowe had extracted himself, all too gladly Midnight was pleased to see, he drew in a deep breath and prepared himself to entertain the shadows once more. With only one oil lamp burning in the room, it did not take long for the familiar sensation of a thousand needles pricking him all at once to envelope him, filling his body seemingly from the inside out and sending his senses into a heightened state of awareness.

Focusing on the face that lay before him on the table, he gently placed a hand on Amelia Prescott's forehead. The coldness of the touch, along with the spongy feel of her puffy skin, repelled him slightly, but he forced himself to concentrate. A tiny sliver of dark power penetrated her brain, searching the dead matter for any remnants of her final memories.

Her body jerked, and her eyes opened, fixing him with a milky stare though he did not see it. His own eyes were closed in concentration as he scoured her mind. Usually, when he performed this dark deed on a fresh corpse, the deceased's memories were fleeting but clear. However, since it had been two and a half weeks since Miss Prescott's untimely demise, the condition of her organs had deteriorated enough to offer up only the merest of visions.

Children running in circles, laughing.

Singing.

Stone steps.

Trees.

Although the images he received were blurred and the sounds muffled, Midnight recognised the scene: Berkeley Square on Christmas Eve. He pushed harder, funnelling more of his dark power into the rotting pulp that used to be her brain. The stench of the gases released by the victim's decay courted his gag reflex, but he forced himself to look deeper for her last memory.

Dimly lit street.

Heels on cobbles... click, click.
Eyes scanning the shadows.
"Hello? Who's there?"
A muffled reply. A male voice.
"Oh. It's you. Hello again."
More muffled speaking, blurred darkness, and flashes of
recognition.
A swish of a long coat, a hat.
An all too familiar moustache.
Fear.
Confusion.
Cold fingers.

Midnight withdrew from Miss Prescott's mind, but the
sense of unease stayed with him, leaving his heart as cold as
the fingers of death he had just felt in the vision. He could not
determine for sure what he had witnessed, but he could not
deny that this woman had, at least, seen and spoken to
someone strongly resembling the inspector.

A tentative knock at the door drew his attention back to
the present.

"Come in, Sergeant Rowe."

The door creaked open, and Rowe's face appeared at the
crack, almost as if he was reluctant to step fully into the
room. "Anything?"

"I can't be sure. The body is too far into decay to glean
very much," he said, skirting the truth somewhat.

"Right," Rowe said, disappointed. "The kids next, then,
eh? They're more recent."

Once again, Rowe extricated himself from the scene,
leaving Midnight alone to discover what he could. Peeling
back the sheet, he felt his stomach lurch at the sight of the
young girl laid out in front of him. For a brief moment, her
petite features reminded him of his daughter, Polly, and his

heart skipped a beat. Such a young life, cruelly cut short, as many were in the poorer parts of the city. With a tenderness only a parent could understand, Midnight removed the note of paper from under her little snub nose and read it aloud.

"I am definitely dead."

The paper smelled like vinegar and something else he did not recognise. The gases emitted from the cadaver's nose would make the message written in invisible ink appear, therefore, in theory, ensuring that the person would not be mistakenly buried alive. Considering the need for a waiting morgue, Midnight was dubious as to the accuracy of this practice.

The girl remained clothed in the rags she had died in; she'd not been stripped and prepared for burial as had Miss Prescott. He wondered if the girl had been displayed in the public viewing room for the 'gawkers,' as Rowe had called them—a truly contemptible way to pass the time, in Midnight's opinion. He could not understand the attraction of spending an afternoon drinking tea and eating cakes whilst waiting to see which one, if any, of the day's corpses would suddenly awaken. Nothing was more abhorrent or disrespectful than to be paraded as a sort of freakish entertainment. These poor victims should be left in peace while they waited to be committed to their eternal rest.

A little bit of dried foam crusted the girl's chin. He removed his handkerchief and wiped it away. Replacing the kerchief back in his pocket, he placed his hand on the little forehead and probed gently at her memories. In complete contrast to the woman's, these were vivid, loud, and alarmingly clear.

Gredge smiling down at her.

Gredge paying her and her brother coppers for a shoe shine and patting them both on the head.

The scene changed to another time.

Gredge standing in front of the little boy, reaching out a hand, and...

Midnight once again felt the freezing touch of death on him. The little girl's body jerked beneath him. He felt her fear and loss as she saw her brother fall lifeless to the floor seconds before she followed him, and the vision faded to nothing.

The last image in Midnight's head was that of his friend and respected colleague, Detective Inspector Arthur Gredge of Scotland Yard, smirking as he took the lives of the two innocent children.

11

MERITON
JANUARY 12TH 1863

"When will Shins come back, Papa?" Polly asked him for what must have been the hundredth time.

"As soon as he is able," Midnight replied. *If he is able.* He added in thought. Polly heaved a sigh. She desperately missed Widdershins, Midnight knew, and he could not bring himself to tell her what had taken place that night at the church. Indeed, he hardly liked to think on it for when he did so, the heavy burden of guilt reared its ugly head. It lay alongside the guilt he felt for Gredge in a companionable and constant herald of accusation, nestled firmly within his conscience. Midnight checked the time on his pocket watch. Rowe would be here at any moment. After the events at the mortuary the previous night, and the shock of Midnight's discovery, they had both agreed to sleep on things before making any rash decisions about what to do next. Although he hadn't managed an ounce of sleep himself, he felt alert and on edge just the same. He checked his watch once again.

"You ain't heard a word I said," Polly said very matter-of-factly.

Midnight looked up at her. "Hmm? Oh. I am sorry, little

one. I am rather distracted this morning, and I am expecting company. Forgive me?"

"S'pose so." She shrugged but regarded him with suspicion.

She was very perceptive for one so young, and he often found that he could not hide things from her for long. But this morning's business was not something he ever wanted her to find out about.

"It is time for your lessons, is it not, Miss Peeps?"

Polly frowned, her lip curling.

"You had better run along now. Don't keep Miss Carmichael waiting."

Polly turned around and walked sulkily away, brushing past Giles as she went.

"Sir, Sergeant Rowe is here to see you. Should I show him into the parlour?"

"No, not here. We shall talk in my study where we cannot be overheard. Thank you, Giles. I'll take it from here."

'Very well, sir." Giles nodded and went to find Mrs Phillips to order a tea tray for his lordship's guest.

Midnight followed him out into the hallway and found Rowe seated on the wooden settle by the front door. The sergeant rose when he spotted Midnight, and by the look of the lad, he hadn't slept much either. The two men merely shook hands and acknowledged each other with a paltry nod. The usual greeting of 'Good morning' seemed wholly inappropriate given the circumstances in which they were meeting. Midnight could find nothing good about this day.

"I cannot bring myself to believe it." Rowe declared. "Why? Why would he do such a thing?"

"I understand how you feel. I am struggling with the concept myself," Midnight admitted.

A weighted silence fell upon them. Rowe starred at the ceiling and began fiddling with a button on his cuff whilst Midnight paced the rug in his study, deep in thought. It was the sergeant who broke the silence first.

"I'm going to have to tell the superintendent something," he said quietly, not looking at Midnight. "He's had me following the boss for long enough now to be wanting a full report. How can I tell him about you? What do I say?"

"You say nothing. You cannot. It will expose me and put my daughter in danger," Midnight implored.

"But we know he killed them. The boss, he killed those poor kids. What am I s'posed to do? I swore an oath to uphold the law, Lord Gunn." The conflict the young sergeant felt was written all over his face, but Midnight could not risk anybody else knowing about his abilities. For, although Branford was aware that Gredge sometimes met with him during an investigation, Gredge had always maintained that he merely consulted Lord Gunn as an expert alienist—a relatively new practice that involved profiling the personalities of murders and criminals. No one in the force— aside from Gredge, who knew the most regarding his abilities, and Rowe, who knew just enough—was aware of the exact role he played in their investigations.

"I understand your dilemma, Sergeant, truly, and you are a credit to Scotland Yard. However, I need to speak to Arthur face to face. I need to see the truth for myself before I let you take action against him." It was not up for debate. Sergeant or not, Midnight would not allow any more threats to those he loved. They had all been through enough these last two years and if this investigation exposed Midnight, he would no doubt be persecuted, hunted like a monster, and then what would happen to Polly? "We will go to him now." Midnight rose and called for Giles to ready his personal carriage.

"What are you going to do when you see him?" Rowe asked.

"Something that he will not like one little bit."

~

"Are you going to let us in, Arthur? It is rather cold out here," Midnight said to the stunned man in the doorway of number thirteen Little Surrey Street.

"What are you doing here?" Gredge directed his question at Sergeant Rowe, not looking at Midnight.

"We need to talk to you, gov," Rowe said.

Gredge then flashed a look at Midnight. "And you? Why are you here?"

"I'm here to help, Arthur."

Gredge started to turn away and close the door but Midnight grabbed hold of his wrist.

"Please, Arthur. It is important."

The inspector sighed and let them both into his home. As he led them through to the front parlour, Midnight could not help but notice the state the little house was in. Despite the clear morning, the curtains above the window remained closed and no lamp burned, enshrouding the room in dank darkness. The fire in the range was unlit; not even a pile of kindling or cold ash filled the grate, indicating that there had been no fire to heat the house or to cook on for some time. Gredge was a mess, unshaven and unkempt. Midnight had never seen him look so unlike himself, and it worried him.

He got straight to the point. "Arthur, I'm not one for dallying as you know. Rowe and I have discovered something, and we need to speak to you about it. I have been to the mortuary. I have seen inside the heads of the victims in the case you were working, and now, it is time to discover the truth, once and for all. I am doing this with or without your permission, so you can protest all you like, but I will not—cannot allow you to stop me. For all our sakes'."

Gredge's eyes widened at this alarming declaration. "What the bleeding hell are you talking about, man? Doing what?"

"You had better sit down, Arthur. I am going to look inside your head."

"Like Hell you are!" Gredge growled, backing away.

Midnight and Rowe flanked him, preventing any chance of escape.

"Why do you want to do that? I told you before, Gunn, you ain't messing around in my bonce. Over my dead body!"

"And it may well come to that, Arthur, if you don't allow me in," Midnight hissed.

"Threats now, is it?" Gredge said. Horrified, he appealed to his junior. "And you, *Sergeant,* you gonna let him get away with this? Call yourself a copper? Pfft!"

Rowe swallowed hard but said nothing, standing his ground.

"If you have nothing to hide, then you have nothing to fear," Midnight said.

Gredge rounded on him. "Oh no? I remember what happened to the last living person you attempted to mess with. She ended up dead!" Gredge spat. "And what are you talking about—'*nothing to hide*'? What is it that you are looking for exactly?"

"The truth," Midnight replied. "When I looked into the minds of those people at the mortuary, I saw who killed them, Arthur. I saw whose eyes they looked into as they perished. Yours."

Arthur Gredge fell heavily back into his old armchair, defeated. His eyes brimming with tears, he shook his head in denial and whispered, "No. You are wrong. You have to be." He looked up at the two men, suddenly unsure. "I... I am not a killer."

12

MERITON

JANUARY 14TH 1863

ℛ∥ℛ

A sort of melancholic sense of grief had settled over Meriton House. Everyone had been shocked and saddened at the news that Detective Inspector Arthur Gredge had walked willingly into Stone's End Police Station on the afternoon of January twelfth and confessed to the murders of Miss Amelia Prescott and the two Barnes children, Vinnie and Violet.

Midnight had spent the last days since then, alone in his basement room. He hadn't eaten but had managed to consume an entire bottle of his favourite French brandy. It still did not seem real— Gredge a killer? The notion was preposterous and yet he had seen it in Gredge's mind.

He had never witnessed a murder from the killer's point of view before, and it had felt distinctly odd to him, almost as if he were looking through frosted glass. Usually, when he ploughed through the memories of the recently dead, they were pretty clear, depending, of course, on the condition of the body and the extent of decay. But this was different.

After many hours of brandy-induced contemplation, Midnight had come to the conclusion that Gredge's memories were somehow obscured as, even though he had confessed —"After all," Gredge had said, "how could your powers be wrong?"—the inspector maintained that he could not recall the events of the evenings in question. Midnight assumed his friend must have blotted the trauma from his mind or that whatever paranormal parasite was possessing him, as Midnight was convinced must be the case, had erased Gredge's mind.

The inspector was now locked up in a secure cell in Surrey County Gaol. He was being held in solitude until the date of his trial; it wouldn't do to let a child-killing copper in amongst the general population. They would tear him apart.

Midnight was indebted to Arthur for keeping his secret. Rowe had pointed out that Superintendent Branford was a spiritual man, a believer of sorts in the unexplained, and he would likely think Midnight's powers as something born of the Devil himself. They had debated for some time as to how to present the evidence of Gredge's guilt without exposing Midnight and his abilities. That is when Arthur had told them that he would confess. That was also when Midnight had made a silent vow to himself that he would get to the bottom of this extraordinary turn of events, if it was the last thing he ever did. For, although he had witnessed the terror and demise of those three innocent people, he had also sensed Arthur's emotions when he'd touched him, and there was nothing of a killer's soul in the man's body. Ergo, he must be possessed or controlled by something, and if that were true, then Midnight was just as responsible for those deaths as anyone.

Alerted by the sound of light footsteps descending the basement stairs to his secret room, Midnight frowned and swung around in his leather captain's chair to ask Giles the reason for the disturbance of his requested solitude. He was surprised to see a nervous-looking Laura emerge, carrying a silver tray with a bowl of something hot and steaming on it.

She cleared her throat. "Beggin' your pardon, Your Lordship, but Mrs Phillips insisted I bring you some chicken soup seeing as you ain't eaten in a while." She fixed him with a shy smile and bobbed a curtsey.

"Thank you, but I am not hungry."

"Mmm. Mrs Phillips said you'd say that so she's told me to tell you that—" She paused, chewing her lip. "—that either you eat it or she'll come down here and spoon feed you herself." This made Midnight's lip twitch, and Laura blushed.

"Did she indeed? Well, then, I supposed you had better set it down on the desk here," he said, moving his chair aside to allow her room to place the tray down and set the bowl of delicious-smelling broth before him.

As she reached for the tray and turned to leave, Midnight stopped her. "How did you get in? I am sure only Giles and Mrs Phillips know of this place."

Laura's cheeks turned even redder. "Mr Morgan let me in. He didn't want to," Laura said quickly. "Only Mrs Phillips said she would box his ears and starch his breeches with itching powder if he didn't let me bring you the food." Laura could not stifle her giggle. It was such a joyous, infectious sound that Midnight could not help but chuckle himself.

"God forbid any of us ever cross dear Clementine."

"Indeed not, sir. She is scary sometimes." Laura laughed, and Midnight felt the darkness leave his heart for one blissful moment. Laura curtseyed and turned to leave once again. And once again, he reached out impulsively to stop her, but she gasped and put her hand in her pocket. "Oh! I forgot to give you this. Mr Morgan said it came in the second post at one o'clock." Laura handed him a letter.

He did not recognise the handwriting on the front, and the

postage mark was local. He opened it, his eyes scanning the page quickly and he smiled.

"Good news, sir?"

"I suppose it is. It will serve as a distraction from this mess, at least."

"You mean the inspector, don't you?"

"I do. I admit that I have been able to think of little else the last two days. Anyway..." He held up the letter. "This is an invitation to see Miss Elldy Bird at the British Museum. She has embarked on some research for me, and it seems she has discovered something interesting."

"Sounds exciting, sir. I ain't never been to the museum meself. Though I should like to, one day."

Midnight waved the letter at Laura. "The invite is for tomorrow. Why don't you come?" he suggested.

"Oh. That's very kind of you, sir, but I... I can't. I have my duties and besides, it... wouldn't be proper."

"Oh. Indeed, yes. I understand, but I shall ask Mrs Phillips to relive you of your duties tomorrow, and you shall take Polly along with you. I was merely suggesting that I take you and my daughter, of course, in the carriage... seeing as I am to go there tomorrow." Now, it was his turn to blush as he realised what Miss Carter had thought he had meant. Just like that, all of the shame he had felt regarding that night with Laura in Samoch Cottage when he had held her hand a moment too long returned. He had almost—

"Then, I would love to. Thank you, Your Lordship. I'm sure Aggie—I mean, Miss Carmichael would enjoy an afternoon off."

"Good grief. Is my daughter really such a rapscallion that her governess needs relief?" he asked with a hint of humour.

"I think we both know the answer to that." Laura grinned.

"Unfortunately, Miss Carter, I am inclined to agree."

13

THE BRITISH MUSEUM
JANUARY 15TH 1863

ЯｌR

P olly jumped down from the carriage as soon as the driver-come-footman, Charlie Fenwick, opened the door.

Miss Carmichael had dressed her in her best town outfit, coat, hat, and boots and had declared that Polly looked like a proper little lady, even if she didn't behave like one, and bade her a merry farewell. To Laura, she had wished her luck, and then, she had gone to her room to write yet another letter of enquiry, regarding her missing brother, to her father in New York.

Midnight alighted from the carriage next and held out his hand to assist Laura.

Dressed in her best woollen dress, grey woollen coat, a bonnet, and leather gloves borrowed from Miss Carmichael, Laura looked as pretty as he had ever seen her. Indeed, he had found it a struggle not to keep looking at her constantly throughout the journey. She was such a distraction that he had begun to wonder if inviting her along was a good idea. At least he had his meeting with Miss Bird to occupy his mind, and he knew that Polly relished Laura's company, so the two of them would enjoy exploring the exhibits together.

"Be off with you both and enjoy the exhibits," he said to the excited pair. "I will come find you once my meeting is over."

Polly gave her father an exuberant hug then took the housemaid's hand. "Oh! Ain't this fun, Laura? What shall we see first?"

Laura grinned, the expression lighting up her entire face in a blissful glow that always made Midnight's stomach jolt. "Everything! Lead the way, Miss Polly."

Laura and the girl hurried off hand in hand, and Midnight realised that the sight of them together brought him such joy that he almost couldn't stand it. He turned and, with a smile in his heart, went to find the museum's curator.

Midnight had made some discreet enquiries after his first meeting with Miss Bird. Curiosity had gotten the better of him, and he had discovered her to be a woman of quite some means. An only child of a wealthy family, she had inherited the family fortune when her parents both perished from influenza. She had then broken off her engagement to David Davenport, the son of another well-to-do family, and bought her way in to a place at Bedford College to study history. She became a patron of the museum and, subsequently, one of the museum's main contributors, funding many overseas trips to negotiate the loan of interesting exhibits. Following that, she had lived happily as a single woman since.

It was unheard of in polite society for a wealthy woman to seek gainful employment. Some ladies volunteered with meaningful foundations or charities. Some did nothing other than what was expected of them as wives or daughters of the well-to-do. Elldy Bird, it seemed, thrived on doing just the opposite. Of course, no one dared call her out on it, because she was old money; her family had been one of the wealthiest and oldest families in the country.

Midnight waited in the corridor adjacent to the curator's office right in front of exhibit number 151: a stuffed brown bear standing on its hind legs, with claws bared and teeth showing in a menacing snarl.

"Now, he would have made quite the challenge," he mused.

"He would've probably had you for dinner," a female voice behind him said.

Midnight turned and smiled, having recognised the voice. "Miss Bird! Good day to you." He held out his hand, and she took it, giving it a hearty shake.

"Good day, Lord Gunn. I am glad that you could make today's appointment. I have some rather interesting news to relate."

"Excellent. Shall we go into your office, then?"

"Unchaperoned?" she said in mock indignation.

"I hardly think that appropriate, sir. Do you?"

"Probably not," he agreed. "But then, some would say a lady of such position wearing pantaloons was hardly appropriate either. However, you don't seem to mind."

"Touché, Lord Gunn. For your information—" She gestured at her attire. "—I'm wearing pantaloons because I rode my bicycle to work. Dresses have a habit of getting caught in the chain. Besides, they're extremely comfortable. Why should men have all the luxury of comfort while we ladies are trussed up like a Christmas turkey?"

The imagery elicited a burst of laughter from him and earned a questioning look from her.

"I'm I'm glad I amuse you, sir. Most gentlemen are quite perturbed by my impropriety."

Midnight recognised the challenge in her eyes and met it.

"I am not most men," he replied, an air of suggestiveness in his voice. He held her gaze for a moment, hoping his eyes conveyed his mirth.

The corner of her mouth tuned up slightly. "I can see that," she said softly. "Shall we?"

She led the way into her office and gestured for him to sit down. As it was in his last visit, the room was filled to bursting with ephemera and her desk was littered with piles of papers and books. One would not call her a tidy person—at least in her place of work, it seemed.

Elldy reached down and opened one of the desk drawers, removing from it the package that Midnight had left in her care some weeks ago. Unwrapping it carefully, she placed it on the desk between them and eyed him curiously.

"Before we begin, might I be blunt?"

"Please, do," Midnight said.

"I've heard rumours about you, Lord Gunn, some of which do not put you in a favourable light. How do you plead?"

"Well that would depend on the charge," he replied, amused.

"It is said that you do not behave quite like the rest of high society."

"One may say the same of you, Miss Bird." He smiled.

"Indeed, they do. However, you are known to shun it completely. You do not answer invitations, and you do not attend balls—nor do you entertain. Indeed, some of the city's elite think you are a true man of mystery."

"Is that a crime?" he chuckled.

"Some would say so," she countered. "When I began research for you on this wonderful little object, I became curious as to how such a man might come to own it, for it is unlike anything I have ever seen. So, I confess that I did a little research of my own into your family."

"And… what did you find?" Midnight asked, a tad warily.

"Not very much, as a matter of fact. I know that your father was successful in his business transactions but that he also kept mostly to himself, and that your mother—"

"Died," Midnight cut in. "My mother died. What is your point, Miss Bird?" He could hardly conceal the slightly irritated tone that crept into his voice.

Unconventional as this woman might be, she was now bordering on rude. Elldy seemed to sense his discomfort, for she leaned forward and, in a placatory voice, pleaded her case.

"Forgive me, Lord Gunn. I do not mean to interrogate you regarding your personal life. It is just that… what I have found out about this—" She picked up the cube and turned it over in her hands, a sudden look of desire in her eyes as if she coveted the artefact. "—makes me wonder just *who* you really are."

Midnight found Polly and Laura exploring one of the upper levels of the museum. They were gawping gleefully at a majestic polar bear in a mock-up of an Artic Circle scene.

"*Ursus maritimus*," he declared, making them both jump.

"Papa!" Polly chastised. "I almost soiled me skivvies!" She put her hand on her chest and breathed in dramatically.

"Polly, sweetheart, must you be so coarse?" Midnight frowned, but there was still a twinkle of amusement in his eyes.

"He's a big one," Laura said, changing tack and directing attention back to the stuffed white giant.

"That he is. He happens to be one of my favourite exhibits. Bears are wildly misunderstood, I fear," Midnight said.

"How so?"

"When people think of bears, this is all they see: a ferocious animal, all teeth and claws and brawn."

"And what do you see?" Laura asked.

"The wilderness personified. Bears are independent, intelligent, solitary creatures that answer to no one. Should I be reincarnated, I should like to be a bear, free to roam wherever I choose and do whatever I please without fear of reproach. Life would be an adventure." His eyes glowed brilliant blue as he smiled up at the bear wistfully.

"I think you are more like the bear than you think, sir." Laura's beaming grin showed that his observation had pleased her greatly.

More surprisingly, however, was his own reaction to having made her happy. It felt...*good,* and he wasn't sure how he felt about that.

They finished the rest of the museum tour in just over an hour. They had walked at a slow pace, and Midnight had relished being so close to Laura away from the conventions that her position in his household demanded. So close was she that he could almost taste the sweet scent of her, feel the heat from her beautiful skin. He longed touch her. The arc of her neck was irresistible; it begged to be kissed.

Damn it all to Hell! he cursed internally. Why couldn't she have been born a lady? Then, he could have perhaps courted her in the proper manner. He thought, then, of what Miss Bird had said about him shunning the usual trappings of his social status.

She was correct, of course. He mostly kept to himself for fear of exposure, but he also could not stand the insular mindset of high society and their collective, misguided sense of entitlement and class superiority. He by far and away enjoyed the company of ordinary folk. Their lives and attitudes were hard but real. After what he had learned from Miss Bird this day, he would give a tonne of figs for an ounce of ordinary at that very moment.

14

BERKELEY SQUARE

JANUARY 15TH 1863

ℛℝ

I t was dark when the carriage pulled to a halt outside of
Meriton House. Polly had not stopped chattering the
entire journey home from the museum.

"Did you see it, Laura? Imagine how strong you would
'ave to be to lift that sword!"

"I did see, and yes, you'd have to be a giant, I reckon."
Laura winked at the little mistress.

"I am very glad to see you enjoyed the outing, Miss
Peeps," Midnight said. "And how about you, Miss Carter?
What did you think of your first trip to the British Museum?"
he asked, genuinely interested.

"Oh, I just loved it, sir. I have never seen such wonders
and mysterious things. Thank you for taking me—us. Much
appreciated. I can't wait to tell Charlie about it."

"I should think poor Charlie has heard more than he can
stomach." Midnight chuckled and exited the carriage. "Isn't
that right, Charlie?" he called up to the driver.

"Every word, twice over." Charlie grinned.

Midnight helped his daughter and housemaid down from
the carriage and closed the door.

"Thank you, Charlie," he said.

"Sir," Charlie replied, doffing his cap. The clopping of horses' hooves rang out into the night as Charlie took the carriage round the back to the small stable yard, where he slept in a little wooden cabin next to his beloved horses.

The three people left on the pavement turned to climb the steps that led the way to Meriton's grand front door. Giles had left a lantern burning in the hallway, and its faint glow shone through the glass pane above the door. Laura took hold of Polly's hand, and the two of them skipped merrily up the stone steps. Midnight pulled out his key, ready to unlock the door, when his senses stirred suddenly.

Someone was behind him.

He turned, and before he even had time to ponder why he had heard no footsteps approach, the entity was upon him.

"Arthur! What are you do—?" He did not finish his sentence before he felt the icy touch of death upon him, just as he had through the memories of the dead in the mortuary.

The cold spread through him at a rapid pace, preventing him from calling out a warning to Laura and Polly. He heard them scream, heard them shouting his name and Gredge's. He forced himself to focus and looked Gredge in the eye, trying to see what madness had taken over his friend. Something was very wrong. In the recess of his panicked mind, he wondered how the inspector had escaped from his prison cell. It did not make sense at all.

He called upon the shadows for help, but they did not come. Desperately, he sought out a source of light to draw upon—anything would suffice. The tenuous glow of a nearby street lamp beckoned, and he reached for it with his mind, willing the light to enter his failing body. Midnight felt the warmth of the little trail of light seep into him. Grateful that at least one of his powers had not failed him, he concentrated on channelling it to his heart, to the place where his friend's fingers appeared to have pierced flesh and bone to wrap themselves around his beating core in an attempt to end him.

The healing light pushed hard at the cold, and Midnight was aware of something exploding out of him. He felt the last tendrils of energy he had disappear, along with the apparition of Arthur Gredge.

As he fell to his knees, his body succumbing to the dark, he felt two pairs of arms around him, catching his fall, two frightened and distressed voices begging him to stay with them. And then, everything went black, and he knew of nothing more.

15

MERITON
JANUARY 18TH 1863

ЯⅡR

L aura was in turmoil. It was the third day since the attack and Lord Gunn was still unconscious and, by all accounts, very ill indeed.

Giles had summoned the doctor on the first night, right after he, Laura, and Agnes had carried him upstairs and lain him on his bed. After an extensive physical exam, the doctor had diagnosed a heart attack. "Likely from the fright," he had concluded. Giles had huffed indignantly at this, and Mrs Phillips had run down to the kitchen to prepare a special tincture that she was convinced would bring the master round. It had not, but they persevered, and now, Laura had taken on the task of nursing him at her own insistence. Giles had suggested they send a telegram to Nurse Carstairs, but Laura had reminded him that, if the master accidentally let loose his powers whilst unconscious, it would be curtains for him and the hospital. It was an unlikely story, but she had insisted upon taking on the role of nurse herself.

That horrible night when she saw the inspector attempting to kill his friend—and almost succeeding—had made her realise that she had feelings for Lord Gunn. It had not been a huge surprise to her; she had always sensed the connection between them. But this had been different. She had been able to suppress her feelings whilst he was alive and well, knowing that propriety was priority. However, in that instant when she thought she had lost him, when she had thought him dead, and she had held him in her arms in street, she had wished with all her heart for just one chance to tell him how she really felt, and then, it had looked like it was too late.

There was a faint knock at the door and Polly entered.

"How is Papa? I have just finished me lessons with Aggie, so I thought I'd visit him before Mrs P calls me down for lunch." Polly stood by the end of the bed and gazed hopefully at her father. "He's no better then?"

"'Fraid not, miss. But I'm sure he'll be up and around in no time, eh?" Laura smiled, trying to reassure the girl. "Come 'ere," she said, opening her arms.

Polly went to her and flung herself into her embrace.

"Now, now, miss. It'll be fine. You'll see. We'll make him better again, eh? All of us. And the master will be as good as new."

"Oh, Laura! I hope so. I ain't never had a father before, and I don't wanna lose him so soon. It ain't fair." She sobbed.

"You ain't going to lose anyone, miss. You hear me? There's me and Mrs Phillips and Mr Morgan all looking after him, and we ain't going to let anything bad happen to him, alright? I promise."

Polly sniffed loudly and wiped her nose on her sleeve. Stepping back from Laura, she said, "We need to find the inspector and make him tell us what he did. Then, we can make Papa better."

"I'm not sure how to, or even if that's a good idea, darlin'. You saw what he did to your father, and even with all his powers, he still nearly died. I don't think he'd want you or anyone else in the house going looking for the inspector. Mr Morgan's in the library now, figuring out how to make him better. Best to leave him to it, eh? I'm sure he'll come up with somethin'." Laura smoothed Polly's hair and gave one of her curls a playful tug as she had seen Lord Gunn do. It made Polly smile.

The little girl sat on the edge of her father's grand bed, swinging her feet. "P'raps I should read him a story? Papa likes it when I read. It might make him wake up," Polly said brightly.

"I think that is a lovely idea." Laura beamed. "Why don't you run and fetch a book, but mind you don't disturb Mr Morgan."

"I won't. I promise." Polly swung herself down from the bed and scampered from the room, leaving Laura alone with her recumbent master.

She gazed upon him in his all-too-silent slumber. He still looked very pale, and every now and then, he would shiver violently as if he were freezing. Despite the roar of the coal fire that burned continuously in the room and the three thick blankets that Laura and Mrs Phillips had tucked in around him, he felt cold to the touch. Laura reached for the cup of hot brandy and herbs that the old housekeeper had brewed up, and put a teaspoon of the liquid to his lips.

"Here you go, Your Lordship. This'll warm your cockles a bit, eh?" Most of the liquid ran down his chin and she hurried to wipe it up. She tried again, this time gently encouraging him to open his mouth with her other hand and tilting the spoon so that the hot toddy trickled on to his tongue. It wasn't much, but at least it was something. She dared not attempt to feed him too much of the drink at once for fear of him choking.

"Sorry. I spilled it. That was clumsy of me," she said to

him. "I ain't never nursed anyone before, see? Don't know what I'm doing, really." Laura laughed softly and rose to put more coal on the fire. She continued to chatter with Midnight in their one-sided conversation as she pottered around his grand bedroom, picking up used napkins and piling the dirty crockery, left over from the dinner Giles had brought her earlier, on to a tray.

"Mum always said I'd make a useless wife. I was never very good at cooking or cleaning. Funny that I ended up working as a maid, eh?" Laura sighed heavily and reclaimed her seat by the bed. "Thank you for taking me to the museum, sir. It was very kind. But then, that's you, I s'pose—always kind." Leaning forward, Laura folded her arms on top of the bed close to Midnight's side and lay her head on her arms so that her face was buried in the blankets.

"Please come back to us," she whispered.

Laura stayed like that, her eyes closed, breathing in the scent of the room and listening to the pop and crackle of the spitting coals until Miss Polly came back.

The girl held up a book to show her. "Got one."

Laura lifted her head and smiled, patting the bedcovers. Clambering up beside her father, Polly prepared to read.

"My father's family name being Pir-rip, and my Ch-ris-tian name Philip, my in-fant tongue could make of both names nothink longer or more ex-ex-pli-cit than Pip. So, I called myself Pip and came to be called Pip."

She paused and wrinkled her nose. "He don't half use a lot of words to say not very much this Mr Dickens, eh?"

"That's how fancy people write, I s'pose." Laura shrugged. "What is the story called?"

Polly turned the book to look at the gold lettering on the spine. "Great Ex-pec-tor-ations, or sommin' like that. It's one

Papa bought me to practice on 'cause he reckons it'll improve me 'elocution' and me readin'.'"

"Your reading really has gotten better, Miss Polly." The little girl beamed at Laura, lapping up the praise. "Carry on then," Laura urged her.

The bedroom settled into a companionable silence as Polly eventually fell asleep beside her father. The afternoon sun had sunk low enough to bathe the room in a spectacular wash of orange. Laura looked upon her two favourite people: Polly—who lay angelic-like with her head on her father's chest, looking like butter wouldn't melt—and Midnight—who was majestic and oozing with presence despite his saporous state. How she loved them both.

Her life here at Meriton had changed her completely. Not just her financial status, although that had been one benefit in working for Lord Gunn—he paid her a more-than-decent wage—but in mind and heart too. Midnight always made her feel like she had value and that she could do anything or be anyone, even if she knew it not to be true in her heart. If she could, she would choose to be a lady of means and influence, free to go where she pleased, and buy the best silks, and visit museums and art galleries whenever she felt like it. She would never have to worry about mending holes in her stockings; she would just buy new ones. In her mind, Laura pictured herself dressed to the nines in a shimmering gown made of the best silk, trimmed with French lace, her hair curled and pinned, jewellery adorning her exposed décolletage... She would host a hundred balls and dine in candlelight with Lord Gunn by her side. If she were a lady, she could have everything.

She smiled ruefully to herself. "A nice dream, Laura Elizabeth Carter, but that ain't ever going to happen. You've done good 'ere, gal. Don't spoil it with silly notions that are way beyond your reach."

She stretched out her arm and lay her hand upon his as a single tear slid down her plump pink cheek and fell upon the white cotton sheets. Her heart was both gloriously full and painfully empty. She felt grateful and satisfied with her lot, and yet, when she looked upon her pretend little family, she could not help but desperately yearn for something that would not, could not ever belong to the likes of her.

The last rays of the winter sun skimmed over Midnight's face, and it reminded Laura of one of the perfectly carved marble statues of some Grecian god that she had seen in the museum. He was beautiful. There was no other way to describe him. He was the most enchanting and excitingly dangerous, fair, and kind, and mysterious human being she had ever seen—so heartbreakingly perfect that, right at that very moment, he didn't even seem real to her. It was almost like he glowed from within. Looking down at her hand on his she was startled to find that he *was,* in fact, glowing. It was not just a fancy of her imagination. There was heat and light emanating from the fingers that were clutched in hers.

Laura watched in awe as Midnight's whole body appeared to luminesce with ethereal brilliance. She dropped his hand and stumbled away from the bed, then was back by his side just as quickly.

"No, no, no! Don't die. Please don't die." Laura yanked hard on the bell-pull three, four times. Her heart raced now. What was happening to him? Is this what death looked like?

Polly awoke and rubbed her eyes. "What's 'appening?" she asked, still half asleep, then sat bolt upright when she noticed her father.

Laura's hands were clasped to her mouth. She wanted to scream so loudly. Instead, she yelled instructions at Polly.

"Run and fetch Mr Morgan! Quickly! I think… he's dying. I think the angels have come for him."

Polly didn't move.

"Go! Hurry! What's wrong with you, girl?"

"Look." Polly pointed at her father. "He's not dying, Laura. He's waking up!"

16

STONES END

JANUARY 20TH 1863

ЯⅠR

O nce Midnight had regained consciousness, he had been able to heal himself almost back to full health. The only trace of what had occurred were five scars in the shape of finger-marks that remained emblazoned and raw on his chest, a bizarre circle around his heart and a constant reminder of the attack by his friend.

Only it had not been Arthur Gredge. He knew that now.

Once the entity had touched him, he had known something was very different. However, his daughter and his housemaid had not. Neither had Giles, who had reported the attack to the police soon after the event, thinking that Gredge might once again be apprehended before harming anyone else.

Whilst Midnight had been unresponsive, Laura, Polly, and Giles had been interviewed that very evening only to be told the next morning that Gredge was still, and always had been, safely locked up in his cell in Surrey County Gaol. The result of this was that Lord Gunn had been 'invited' to attend an interview at the station with Superintendent Branford as soon as he was fit and well.

Midnight settled into the chair that Branford offered him, exchanging pleasantries, as good manners demanded. Once the formalities were out of the way, a momentary silence, charged with tension, developed between the two gentlemen.

Branford blinked first. "I am glad to see you are well enough recovered to attend today's meeting, Lord Gunn. Thank you for taking time out from your busy schedule to help us clear this matter up."

"Thank you, Superintendent Branford. Anything I can do to help," Midnight stated.

Branford cleared his throat. "I would like to begin by reading over a brief timeline of events in accordance with the statements given at the time by one Miss Laura Elizabeth Carter and your adopted daughter, Miss Polly Gunn, if I may?"

Midnight proffered a brief nod of acquiescence. and the Super continued. Bending his head over a small pile of handwritten papers on his desk, he read, "On the night of January the fifteenth, an attack upon your person took place in the street outside of your home, Meriton House, Berkeley Square. Is this correct?"

"It is."

"You had just arrived back home with your carriage after an outing to the British Museum with the aforementioned Miss Carter, your... housemaid, and your daughter?"

"That is correct," Midnight replied, choosing not to elaborate as to the reason why Laura had been with them despite the definite emphasis Branford had placed upon the word 'housemaid'.

"I see," Branford said after it became clear that Midnight was offering up not a wink of an explanation to satisfy his curiosity.

Whatever Branford's status was in the force, Midnight

had no intention whatsoever of discussing his private business with this man. Neither would he tolerate intrusive, irrelevant, and impertinent questions.

"In your own words, can you describe to me what happened next?" Branford persisted.

"I will do my best. I helped my two companions down from the carriage. Then, Mr Fenwick, my resident driver and groom, drove the carriage away. I reached for my door key as we, all three, approached the front steps. I felt a sudden presence behind me, and the next thing I remember is waking up in my bed with a very sore head."

"I was hoping for a little more detail, in truth. Can you tell me more about your attacker? Did you recognise him?"

"Him? I confess I have no recollection of the incident other than what I have already described to you. I understand that my daughter and Miss Carter named Detective Inspector Gredge as the man who attacked me, but obviously, we know that to be impossible, seeing as he is safely imprisoned."

"Yes. It is a conundrum, is it not?" Branford raised an eyebrow. "You must have seen his face though. Your housemaid has stated that you even said the detective's name out loud, which means you must have seen the man."

"I am quite sure that Miss Carter's statement is correct. Perhaps I did see the blackguard. However, as I have already told you, I do not now recall," Midnight lied.

Branford tapped his fingers on the desk. "Well, since you declare that Mr Gredge could not possibly be the culprit, given his current situation, I wonder, sir, if you could tell me of any enemies you may have accrued over time or if you can think of anyone who may wish you harm." Branford tried another angle.

Where would you like me to start? Midnight thought to himself. "None that immediately come to mind," he said.

Branford began riffling through the papers on his desk. When he found what he was looking for, he held it up for Midnight to see. "Lord Gunn, I am aware that, for quite some time now, you have acted as a consultant to the Yard, working specifically with and at the personal recommendation of Mr Gredge on some of our more unusual cases."

"I have indeed. It is a privilege to do my part in keeping the citizens of the city safe." Midnight smiled.

"Mmm," said Branford. "You call yourself an 'alienist,' is that correct? You claim to be an expert in this field. I have to say your track record with us is quite impressive."

"Kind of you to say. Thank you. I would not ever proclaim to be an expert in anything. I rather think that overly complimentary label may be due to the inspector's gracious elucidations of my contributions to the investigations we have worked on together."

"Quite," Branford agreed. "And so, Lord Gunn, how would you describe what it is you do for us exactly?"

"I consult."

Branford's eyebrow twitched. He changed tack again. "How would you describe your relationship with Mr Gredge? Would you call him a friend? I refer to an incident earlier this year when Mr Gredge came to your aid when your daughter was kidnapped in Scotland—something a close friend would do. Would you say you know Mr Gredge well?"

Midnight eyed the superintendent quizzically. "I should like to know the relevance of the question to the attack. We have already established that the inspector could not be the culprit of that particular crime, have we not?"

"Being innocent of one crime does not absolve him of another," Branford stated.

"Indeed. However, I am not here to pass judgement on a friend who may or may not be guilty of murder."

"He confessed, Lord Gunn."

"I am aware of that. However, I am also aware, as I am sure you are, that, in this country, a person must be proven to be guilty in a court of law. Should you wish to follow this particular line of questioning, then I would ask that my solicitor be present as is my right, *Mr* Branford. I must confess that I was under the impression we were here to discuss an assault on my person, an attempt on my life, not to pass sentence on a man still awaiting trial. If I am mistaken then please allow me some time to contact my solicitor, and we can reconvene this *meeting* at another mutually agreeable time."

"Sir, I am—" Branford paused, sighed, and pushed himself back in his chair. Looking at the ceiling, he continued. "I have known Arthur Gredge for many years. Had you asked me but a year ago if he was capable of cold-blooded murder, I would have thought you insane. But lately…" He shook his head. "He's changed. In these last months, in particular, I have noticed a vast difference in his countenance and his professional conduct. Elevated, it seems, since his return from Scotland… with you." Branford paused for effect. "Lord Gunn, I would not be doing my job if I did not ask all the right questions."

"All the right questions in all the wrong ways. I understand," Midnight said, nodding. "I understand perfectly." He could see now what Branford was really hoping for; he wanted to see for himself what kind of man the mysterious Lord Midnight Gunn was and how much influence he may hold over Gredge.

In a way, Midnight took comfort in this as it showed that Branford did not truly see Gredge as just a cold-blooded killer. No, he was trying to establish if Midnight was the cause of his best detective's uncharacteristic behaviour.

Midnight had to admit, it was a credit to the superintendent to not take Gredge's confession as gospel.

"I will say this, Superintendent. I do not believe Arthur Gredge committed those murders. I admit to having a few doubts as to that fact before, but as you so graciously accord me, I am an expert of sorts in alienism, as you call it, and Arthur is my friend as well as my colleague. Whether you allow it or not, I intend to use all of my influence to prove him innocent and determine the identity of the real killer. I should like to think that you desire that same outcome."

Branford nodded once.

"Excellent," said Midnight. "Then, rather than fishing in my pool of existence, how about we help each other in this case? I will do my thing, and you will do yours?"

"Alright. I agree. And you will keep me informed of any conclusions you may come to?" Branford asked.

"I will, if you will grant me the same courtesy. You can liaise with me via Sergeant Rowe; he and I are acquainted."

Branford took his time in replying. Tapping his fingers on his desk, he appeared to be deep in thought. Midnight stood and held out his hand for Branford to shake.

Come on, man. Take my hand, Midnight willed the man in his mind.

Finally, the super rose slowly and purposefully from his seat and clasped Midnight's hand.

"Agreed."

At the very moment their skin made contact, Midnight knew that Superintendent Robert Branford was lying.

17

SURREY COUNTY GAOL
JANUARY 21ST 1862

He had at least been allowed some paper and a stick of charcoal to write with, which provided some sense of relief if not comfort. Arthur was having trouble keeping his thoughts straight these last few days, and found that the only way to stop himself from going completely insane was to write them down. He did not have his latest journal with him —no personal possessions were permitted—but the paper and charcoal would suffice. The blackened stick in his hand had worn down to almost half its original size in the short time he had been incarcerated.

Arthur finished the sentence he had been writing and placed the stick carefully back on the piece of brick that stood askew in the wall by the small window of his cell. He held his scribblings up to the candle to read.

"Gredge! You got a visitor."

Startled by the gaoler's rough shout, Arthur jumped.

"You got ten minutes," he heard the man say.

Then, another, more familiar voice pierced the gloom. "Let us say I have as long as this buys me, shall we?" Gredge heard the chink of coins, and the gaoler chuckled.

"Take as long as you want, Your Lordship. It ain't like he's goin' anywhere… not yet anyway." The gaoler shuffled away, heavy iron keys clanking at his belt.

Gredge's heart beat faster in hopeful anticipation as a graceful but imposing figure emerged from the gloom. "Midnight?"

"Hello, Arthur. I shan't ask how you are. I can see it for myself. You look dreadful."

"What are you doing here?"

"A pleasure to see you, too. I gather, then, that now we are done with the niceties, we can get straight down to business?"

"Eh? What business?" Gredge walked closer to the iron bars that sealed him away from the world.

"Proving your innocence, of course. I'm not here to broker a sale, man."

"My…" Gredge frowned. "But… you said… you saw. In my head that I—"

"I was wrong, Arthur, so very wrong, and for that, I offer you my most humble apology."

"Lay still, will you? I cannot concentrate while you are fidgeting so."

"Are you sure you're not just wasting your time? I still don't understand how you could be wrong," Arthur protested as he wriggled under Midnight's touch.

Exasperated, Midnight let go of his friend's head and addressed him as if he were a rebellious child. "Look, here. We can do this with you conscious or unconscious—it is entirely up to you. But if we are to do this, it needs to be now, before the guard returns and finds me in here with you in an unlocked cell. The way you are behaving, anyone would think that you want to hang. Now, will you please be quiet and let me in?"

"Fine!" Gredge hissed and went rigid on his rickety bed. "Just… be bloody careful. My bonce is messed up enough as it is."

"Shush!" Midnight hissed back.

Gredge grumbled something under his breath and closed his eyes.

Midnight put his hands back on Arthur's forehead and drank in the shadows. Flashes of imagery and sounds raced through his mind's eye as he dug deeper and further back in time into Arthur's memories. He pushed until he found memories of Scotland, the hill, the stone circle, Shins, the blue glow of the portal.

Midnight drew in a little of the candlelight to balance himself; experience told him not to let the shadows gain too much purchase in his mind. Thin tendrils of golden light seeped into him, and he mixed their warmth in with the smokey darkness.

Slowly, Midnight brought the memories forward to more recent times, pausing each time he thought something looked promising. But he could not find anything other than evidence of the mental struggles his friend had suffered these last months. That was until he skimmed the memory of his and Arthur's trip to the archives at the museum.

Midnight focused hard and slowed the flourish of images down to normal speed. He used his abilities to read emotions when in contact with a person to try and sense what Gredge had been feeling then. As his mind's eye merged with Gredge's, he began to see and feel things as if he *were* his friend.

Boredom, dusty shelves, dim lighting.

Curiosity, a wooden mask, runes.
Claustrophobia.
Can't breathe!
Need to get out!
Help me!

Midnight had the sense of falling, the sound of something crashing nearby and smashing. His vision began to darken, and he saw himself then, through Arthur's memories, rushing towards him, along with Elldy Bird.

Midnight pushed on to the moment when Arthur came to—

This! This feels different. Arthur feels different.

"It is the mask! Arthur? Are you alright? I think I know what has happened to you."

"Midnight?"

"Yes?"

"Do not ever, ever do that to me again."

18

THE BRITISH MUSEUM
JANUARY 21ST 1863

ЯⅡR

Midnight knew he was not the most patient person, and waiting to speak to the museum's curator—as he had turned up without making an appointment first—was proving rather difficult. He knew it was late in the afternoon. He knew it was a long shot. But he had to try. Time was of the utmost importance now that Gredge had named the date of his trial as February first. That left Midnight just ten days to prove Gredge's innocence.

In truth, he had not yet worked out how he was to convince a judge and jury that some supernatural entity had likely possessed the good inspector and driven him to murder. Midnight would get to that later. Right now, he needed to talk to Elldy Bird.

He checked his pocket watch again. It was just twenty minutes to four o'clock, when the museum would be closing for the day.

"Damn it all to Hell and back!" Midnight cursed under his breath.

"Lord Gunn? To what do I owe this late, and unexpected pleasure?"

Midnight spun around, embarrassed to have been caught using such brash language in front of a lady, and in a public place no less.

"Miss Bird. My apologies on all accounts. I beg your pardon for the intrusion, but I need to talk with you on a very urgent matter."

"So urgent that it cannot wait until tomorrow? Why, what on earth could you need from a museum curator at such short notice?"

"I need access to the room in the basement, the one near the archives. There is an artefact in there that I believe has made Detective Inspector Gredge—the man who accompanied me on my first visit?" he clarified after seeing her confusion.

"Ah, the bumbling fool who broke one of the museum's oldest treasures!"

"He did? Oh, I am sorry. Perhaps I can make a donation to the museum on his behalf?"

"Perhaps. Get to the point of your visit, sir. The museum is about to close, and I have much to do."

"Quite. As I was saying, there is an artefact in that room that has made my friend very sick, and I must see it. Please?"

"But... that is impossible!" Miss Bird blurted out.

"It may sound that way, but I assure you it is not."

"No. You misunderstand me, sir. I can clearly see that you believe what you are saying, and there is no doubt of the sincerity and urgency in your manner. And as much as I would love to oblige you, I am afraid it is impossible today, at least."

Midnight checked his time piece once more. "The museum does not close for another fifteen minutes. Surely, there is time for a quick visit."

"I am sorry, Lord Gunn. The museum may not close until

four. The archives, however, close every day at three o'clock, and I do not have the key."

"You are the curator," Midnight quipped.

"Yes. However, in the interest of maintaining the security of everything stored within the archives, I do not hold the key. In fact, there is a rota; the designated key holders change monthly—another safety measurement. There are some extremely rare and valuable documents in that room," she explained. "I am afraid you will have to come back tomorrow. Unless there is anything else I can help you with."

Midnight could not hide his disappointment, but then he had a flash of inspiration.

"Actually, Miss Bird, there is. Upon my last visit, when we discussed my cube. You said you had kept notes on the research you had completed. Do you still have them?"

"Of course. I always keep my research. One never knows when it might be useful."

"Indeed." Midnight smiled. "I wonder if I might borrow those notes? I assure you I will return them as soon as I have finished with them."

Elldy frowned but agreed. "They are notes on the research that you paid me for, sir. I suppose you are entitled to borrow them. Wait here, and I shall bring them to you." She returned a few moments later with bundle of documents tied with ribbon and handed them to Midnight. "Do try not to lose them."

"Thank you, Miss Bird. You have been most helpful." He turned to leave, but Elldy called out to him.

"See you soon, Lord Gunn. I look forward to your return and your very large donation!"

"Oh, I do intend to return, Miss Bird," he replied then, to himself, said, "Much sooner than you think."

19

THE BRITISH MUSEUM
THE EVENING OF JANUARY 21ST 1863

ℛ∥ℛ

I t was fully dark by four thirty. Midnight had waited in a tea shop not far from the museum on Great Russell Street. By five o'clock, most of the museum staff had gone home. Elldy Bird had left at five-twenty-five. Midnight calculated that the only remaining staff must be the nightwatchmen and perhaps a few cleaners who worked the evenings, clearing away any mess left behind by the museum's patrons.

He tucked the bundle of papers that Elldy had loaned him into his coat pocket and prepared to scale the iron railing that ran the perimeter of the site. Checking first that there was no other person in sight, he sought out a safe place to climb. He did not want to use his powers to assist him in case a passerby happened upon him; scaling the barrier in a normal fashion he could explain, whereas using his powers to elevate himself up and over it he could not. However, the night was clear and crisp, and even dressed in dark clothing as he was, the bright gas lamps made him all-too visible.

"Perhaps a little cover would not do any harm," he muttered.

Opening his palms, he sent small flurries of smokey dark power outwards and upwards until the street lamps became shrouded in gloom, dimming the street where he stood enough to camouflage his climb over the railing. As soon as he reached the grand stone steps at the museum's entrance, he let the shadows by the lamps go and redirected them towards the locked doors in front of him.

The dark tendrils whirled and swirled inside the keyhole until he heard a distinct click. Grasping the handle, Midnight gently turned it and pushed open the door just enough for him to squeeze through.

Once inside, he gathered his bearings—not easy in the gloom of the big building. There were faint voices up ahead.

Nightwatchmen!

Standing as still and as quiet as he was able, he listened to see if he was at any risk of being discovered. Deciding it was clear, Midnight slowly made his way through the darkened halls, past the glass display cases that housed the exhibits until he found the stairway that led to the storage basement.

The stairwell held the same fusty smell of decay as it had before, and it was as black as the Devil's soul with none of the oil lamps lit. Even when his eyes had adjusted to the faint glow of moonlight that managed to seep in through one small window, it was impossible to see anything.

"I need a damned light." Fumbling his way down the staircase, he felt around for the small desk that he remembered had been nearby and found an oil lamp atop it. After more fumbling, he managed to find a box of long matches. He took one out and struck it. The small flickering flame became a larger one once the lamp was lit, and the enclosed walls seemed to creak in welcome of it.

Now beyond the basement door, the heels of Midnight's shoes clicked loudly on the flagstone floor, making him feel rather exposed despite the many towering shelves in the storage room, and bulky artefacts that were shrouded in ghostly white protective sheets.

He found the spot on the floor where Arthur had fallen, and walked down the aisle from which his friend must have emerged. Stopping to look and rummage around the vast collection of objects, he found the mask he had seen in Arthur's memory.

Placing the lamp on the shelf, Midnight held the mask in his left hand, making sure that its wrappings remained as a protective barrier between the artefact and his bare flesh. From what Arthur's memory had shown him, the inspector had put the mask to his face and then had immediately felt ill. Bringing it closer to the light, Midnight carefully turned the mask around, looking at every inch for any sign of a curious marking or poisonous residue that might explain his friend's sudden and bizarre reactions. He saw nothing but the engraved runes on the front-side metalwork.

"There has to be *something*," he said insistently.

He felt sure from his vision that this strange, Nordic artefact was somehow responsible for Gredge's uncharacteristic killing spree.

There was a sudden noise at the top of the steps.

"Bleedin' door's unlocked!" One of the nightwatchmen declared.

"Eh? Can't be. Ernie locked up today. He'd never leave it open," said another.

"Shall we go down and 'ave a look, then?" the first man asked half-heartedly.

There followed a few seconds of silence in which Midnight held his breath and clutched the mask to his chest as if trying to prevent it from making any noise.

"Nah. Just close the door, and we'll tell Ernie in the

morning. Ain't like anyone's down there now. Fancy a cuppa? It must be time for a sit down by now, eh?"

"There's a light," the other man said in a hushed tone.

"Eh? You sure? Let me see."

Midnight silently cursed and quickly smothered the lamp's glow in a cloud of shadow.

"You're seeing things, Dickie. There's nothin' there. You been on the pop again?"

Relived, Midnight heard the clang of the door closing, and the faint voices of the two men's conversation fade into nothing.

Alone once more, he let the light breathe again and examined the mask a second time. How frustrating. He had been convinced the mask would show some evidence of what exactly had caused harm to Gredge.

Deciding in a moment that the only sensible thing to do was to 'borrow' the artefact and study it at length and in detail at home, Midnight carefully bound the wrappings around it and stuffed it under his coat.

No one noticed him leave—the gentleman thief. No one except the man in the long coat and tweed cap.

20

MERITON

LATE EVENING, JANUARY 21ST 1863

Throwing his coat over the rack in the hallway, Midnight made straight for the library, shouting for Giles as he went. "Bring me everything you can find on Norse mythology, the Icelandic sagas, Scandinavian folklore, runes, *anything!* I'll be in my study. And Giles?"

"Sir?"

"Don't forget the brandy, we are going to need it."

~

Some hours later, when the fire had almost burned down to nothing but ash, Midnight finally found a passage in one the many books in his father's old collection.

"Here! Giles, look. I think I have found something." Sliding the book across the desk to where Giles sat, surrounded by open tomes and piles of old papers, Midnight tapped the page he had been reading. "Right there. What do you think?"

Giles turned the book around so he could read from the

place on the page that Midnight had shown him. "Bind runes: a combination of two or more runic symbols conjoined to make a single glyph of significant power and meaning."

"I believe this is why the markings on this mask are proving difficult to translate. These are not like any runes I have seen in any of these books. They are very stylised, almost ornamental. No wonder I did not recognise them. Usually bind runes are made up of just two, sometimes three, single runes but these have more." He held up the mask to demonstrate. "See this one, for example? It is faded, but I can certainly determine there to be at least four or five from the Elder Futhark—the oldest form of Scandinavian runic alphabets.

"Giles, I have seen something very similar on my cube! Miss Bird wrote many research notes on it. I have them here in my desk." Midnight rummaged around in his draw for the notes.

"Who is Miss Bird, and of what cube are you referring to, sir?"

"Ah, yes, of course! I have not told you; a few months ago, I found something in the attic. It is an ancient cube made of wood and metal. There was no reference to it in Father's inventory, so I took it to the curator at the British Museum—a woman no less! Can you believe that? Admirably progressive! Never mind; I digress. Miss Bird has been researching its origins, and she loaned me her research notes. She told me some erm… *interesting* things, shall we say, about the artefact and to whom it supposedly belonged."

"I see. And you believe this to be of use to us how exactly?" Giles asked in a sudden and inexplicably cautious tone.

"Give me a moment, and I will show you. The cube is in my room." Midnight sprang from his chair and strode across his study to the bookshelf that hid the passageway to his secret room. Pulling out the false book that unlocked the door, he tapped his foot impatiently as the bookcase swung open to reveal the entrance. He was about to venture inside when he paused. "Something is wrong."

"I am with you, sir," Giles declared as he rose and went to his master's side.

The normally darkened stairwell was awash with an unearthly blueish light that appeared to be emanating from Midnight's room. Wary, he reached out with his senses but could feel nothing malignant, just a strong sense of magical energy.

"Shins!"

It had to be the return of the mutt. He must have found a way back somehow. Polly would be delighted. As he and Giles descended the worn stone steps, the feel of the energy became more discernible, and he realised then that it was not the same as the energy he had felt from the portal.

When they reached the bottom of the stairs and turned the corner into the basement room, Midnight discovered the source of the light.

"The cube. It is glowing!"

"Has it ever done that before?" Giles asked.

"No. Not that I am aware of."

"Do not touch it!" Giles cried as Midnight reached for it. "You do not know if it is safe."

Midnight considered the object a moment, his brows wrinkling in thought. "I think it is, Giles. I cannot describe what I am sensing, but I do not feel threatened in any way. I think I am meant to touch it."

Giles knew his master well enough to know that he did not need to question his actions again; if Lord Gunn sensed no danger, then he trusted there to be none.

Midnight gathered in to himself a small dose of dark power, just in case his senses were off as they had proven so with Gredge, and reached out to pick up the mysterious cube.

The moment he held it in his hand, it began to throb. A rhythmic pulsing coursed through his hand and through his arm, it was as if the cube had become a physical extension of his own limb. He turned it over in his hand and saw that the strange glyphs that were engraved around the outside were glowing also.

From the study above, someone screamed and a second later came a clattering and the sound of china breaking. Giles and Midnight, who still held the cube, raced up the stairs to find a very frightened and flustered Clementine Phillips, surrounded at her feet by the smashed contents of the tea tray she had obviously been bringing to them. Her face was frozen in fear, her mouth open in a wide and perfect O.

There, on the desk in Midnight's study, the stolen mask levitated, spinning around slowly. It glowed with the same spectral blue light as the object in Midnight's hand.

Giles pulled his attention away from the strange sight and went to the aid of Mrs Phillips. Midnight stared in fascination at the two artefacts that appeared to be linked somehow. How could that be so? The mask had been stored in the museum's basement for who knows how long, and the cube had been hidden away in the attic at Meriton for at least two decades, maybe more. Midnight had no idea if his father had even known about the cube, or if he had, how long it had been since the box had been opened and the cube had seen the light of day.

The pulsing in his hand became more rapid and the cube began to vibrate. The blueish glow of the runes upon it flared white-hot, and a high-pitched whine burst forth from it. The corners of the cube suddenly popped open, spilling more blinding light into the room forcing Giles and Mrs P to shield their eyes. Midnight dropped it on the floor and stumbled backwards.

The moment the cube hit the floor, everything went quiet. The light vanished, and the sound disappeared. The mask dropped back onto the desk where it had been placed before, and the two objects lay still and benign. Nothing except the heavy panting of the three shocked people in the study could be heard.

"I did tell you not to touch it." Giles could not help himself. He had his arms wrapped protectively around the shaking housekeeper.

Midnight looked at his butler and frowned slightly. Something in Giles' tone and manner was off. The old man was angry—no... frightened, and Midnight had to wonder why. He and Giles had faced worse things over the years than a magical box.

"Giles? Is there something you are not telling me?"

The old butler glanced at the cube on the floor.

"You should have told me what you found. I could have helped you. I could have told you—" He stopped himself before he said any more.

Midnight's heart was beating hard against his chest. Something was not right. Convinced Giles was holding back, he asked, "Could have told me what, Giles? What do you know?"

After what seemed forever, Giles replied, "I know nothing other than you are stupidly spontaneous and downright irresponsible at times, Master Midnight. Your father, he... entrusted your safety to me. How am I to keep my promises to him if you continue to place yourself in danger?" Giles stepped away from Mrs P, whose mouth was agog still but now with shock at the anger in her old companion's voice.

"*Mister Morgan!*" she cried. "Really. That is no way to speak to the young master, now, is it? We've all had a shock, it's true. Now, I suggest you help me clean up this mess and come and have a sit down in the kitchen with me," she instructed. "You and I have some discussing to do."

JOURNAL ENTRY OF ARTHUR GREDGE

JANUARY 1863

T he date of my trial draws near, I am told, although I choose not to keep track of the days. Many before me have marked their time on the walls of this prison cell, and I find myself tracing their etchings with my fingers, wondering how many of them died... as I am told I will if I am found guilty.

I sit in this grey filth and fight with myself to remember. My mind is addled, I am sure, for I seem to drift in and out of lucidity. My gaoler tells me I mutter in my sleep, but I do not ever recall laying down. I am plagued by chills and a voice in my head that I do not recognise, yet claims to be me.

I do not know how I have come to be so alone and so fallen. Midnight has visited me twice, as has Sergeant Rowe, though I do not think he will come again. The lad seemed as though he felt obliged to visit rather than wanted to. He asked a lot of questions about Midnight. I'm not sure why. Perhaps he intends to take my place once I am gone.

Sometimes I think I see myself, late into the night when all are sleeping, standing on the other side of the bars. I sit and look at the ghost of who I will soon become. My apparition *smiles at me, and I smile back, welcoming the peace it promises after the inevitable end to this nightmare I am living.*

I think of my home and my desk in my office, the walks in the park, and the dog that I always wanted but now shall never have. It seems like another life.

I am told by my gaoler that I have not been here that long but it already feels like a lifetime. I cannot focus for long, and so I try to write my thoughts down whenever I have a lucid moment.

Midnight tells me he is sorry and that he feels responsible for my state of mind, but it doesn't matter. I chose to be his friend. I recruited his help in my special cases. I have brought this madness upon myself. He also vows to absolve me of any guilt, but I do not see how he can.

I have a vague recollection of talking to the boy I killed at the docks. He shined my shoes. I also now remember the young woman who offered me a cigarette on Christmas Eve outside the house on Berkeley Square. I had cut my hand on the wall, and it was bleeding. She gave me her handkerchief to wrap around the wound. I deserve no mercy or kindness. I must have killed those poor people. Although, I still do not recall. What other explanation could there be?

I wish I was out there. I am sure I could seek a solution as to why my mind and conscience have turned against me. I was not born a killer... and yet here I am.

21

AN UNEXPECTED DEVELOPMENT
JANUARY 25, 1863

ℛ∥ℛ

"What is it, Miss Peeps? I know you are there, so you may as well come out," Midnight said without looking up from his desk.

He heard the rustle of silk and then a little voice spoke out. "Papa? Are you alright? I came to see you 'cause you ain't been to read me a story or nothin' for two days. Miss Aggie said you was very busy and not to disturb you but…"

"But you thought you would anyway?" He finished and looked up from his desk, smiling.

"You look terrible! Did you know?"

"I do now." Midnight chuckled. "I am sorry I have not been by to read you story. That is unforgivable of me. Miss Carmichael is right though; I am very busy trying to help our friend."

"Yeah, I know. Do you think you can help the inspector? 'Cause I don't think he deserves to 'ang. I like him," Polly said simply.

Midnight beckoned to the girl, and she hurried over to him. He wrapped her in a warm embrace and spoke into her hair. "I am trying my very best. That I can promise you, darling."

"Do you need any help, Papa? I'm gettin' really good at reading. Maybe I can help you with your books and all?"

"That is very kind of you, Polly, but this is something that I need to do on my own." He smiled.

Giles entered the study. "Sir, you have a visitor. A miss Elldy Bird from the British Museum. Should I let her in?"

Midnight palmed his face. He had no time for this right now, but he did not see how he could refuse.

"Yes. Please show her to my study, would you, Giles?"

"Of course, sir. Should I… send for tea? If you don't mind me saying, Miss Bird appears to be rather… put Out."

Midnight smirked. "Oh, I am sure she is. Yes, do send Mrs P up with a tray. Thank you." He turned to his daughter. "Well, Miss Peeps. It seems you must run along and find your governess. Papa has business to discuss." He hugged her and tugged her curls. "I promise that I will come and read to you this evening, alright? And if I do not, you have my permission to put salt in my tea for a week," he teased.

This made Polly giggle as she was leaving. A few moments later, Giles ushered a flustered looking curator into his study. Midnight rose to greet her. She did not look pleased.

"Save me the pleasantries, please, Lord Gunn. I think you know why I am here."

"Miss Bird. How nice to see you. Sit down."

"I am going to get straight to the point, Lord Gunn. You came to see me regarding access to the basement archives a few days ago. Am I to assume that the subsequent disappearance of a certain Norse artefact from said basement is merely coincidence?"

Midnight opened his mouth to reply but was interrupted.

"Please, sir. Do not presume to insult me by denying it. I know for a fact that Ernie locked up that room, and I also recall your very insistent visit that same evening requesting access due to some emergency you claimed to have been involved in." She paused and regarded him for a moment. "You know what I discovered during my research. You have my notes. Do not play games with me, Lord Gunn. I am here for the explanation I deserve. You will tell me what I want to know, or I will make my report to the police regarding the theft of museum property."

Silence settled in the room for a moment while Midnight decided upon a course of action. Miss Bird seemed to be a person of morals. She certainly was not one to suffer fools, that much was clear.

"You are correct," Midnight said, deciding on some semblance of truth, at least for now. "I did *borrow* an item. As I said before, when I came to you for help, it was very important. So important, in fact, that it became a matter of life or death. I had to have access to that artefact in order to save my friend's life. Is that a good enough explanation for you, Miss Bird?"

"No. Not really, but it is a start. Do continue." She fixed him with a grim glare as if daring him to provoke her.

"During our last meeting, you asked me many questions, did you not?"

"I did."

"You asked me who I am. Well, Miss Bird, allow me to enlighten you?"

"I am listening."

"I… am the son of Josiah and Josephine Gunn. I own a vast fortune. I keep to myself. I am building a hospital for the poor people of London. I… know things, and I have special *abilities,* you could say. I help out Scotland Yard in some of their most unusual cases—mostly pertaining to the supernatural or unexplainable—top secret sort of things, you know. My friend and colleague, Inspector Gredge, who you met, has been accused of three murders that I know he did not commit, and I am on a mission to prove that he is indeed innocent. Your ancient artefact is integral to my investigation. I am humbly asking you now to allow me to continue with my endeavours to save the life of my very dear friend, Arthur Gredge. Is *that* enough of an explanation for you?"

Elldy regarded him for a while before answering. "It will do, for now. I am no fool, sir. There is much more to you than meets the eye. You may find that to be true of both of us in fact. But that is a discussion for another time. Now, what can I do to help?"

"You want to help?" Midnight said, a little taken aback.

"From what you say, it does not look I will be getting my mask back until you have helped the good inspector, and I am somewhat of an expert in history so…" She shrugged.

"You do understand that there are things I cannot discuss with you? I need to maintain a certain—"

"Façade?" Elldy cut in.

"Public image," Midnight corrected.

"Lord Gunn, you do not need to tell me anything you do not wish me to know. Indeed, there are some things I am happier not knowing. However, what I do know is that an innocent man is relying on you to free him, and I would like to help you."

Midnight fixed her with a broad grin and pushed a pile of books towards her. "Well, in that case, Miss Bird, you had better get started."

22

ᛞᚱᚨᚢᚷᚱ ᛞᛟᛟᚱ

JANUARY 25TH 1963

ᚱᛁᚱ

"This one here is called Othala, and according to this book, it is representative of one's sacred ancestral home or land. It also makes the phonetic sound 'oh,' and since we have two of them, the second word so far is D-O-O," Midnight said.

"I think we can safely assume the second word is door. Do you not think?" Elldy asked. "Best to check it, though. I have a feeling it might be important to translate these runes as thoroughly as possible."

"I agree. It seems this one means wheel, and it is supposed to help the wearer focus on one single thing at a specific time and place. Is any of this making sense to you at all?" Midnight said.

"Let us recap on what we have, shall we? We now know that this whole line of glyphs here, across the brow of the mask, reads, 'Draugr Door'. We know the general meanings of each rune. And this means we should be able to determine exactly what the bind runes mean also."

"By the same rule, we can translate the rest of the bind runes on my cube and add to the research you have already completed. However, I think the next step, before we go on, is to find out what a Draugr Door is. I do not want a repeat of what happened before, when these two objects were triggered somehow—not until I understand them at least."

"What happened before?" Elldy enquired, her natural curiosity piqued.

"It is probably better not to ask."

"Ah! One of those need-to-know situations, perhaps?"

"Indeed. Just trust me when I say that you do *not* need to know that."

"Do I need to know how you believe that this mask hurt your friend? Am I in danger if I touch it?"

"No, I don't believe so. As long as you don't put it to your face. That is what Arthur did just before he fell ill."

"I see. I must then assume, since we have tested the artefact for potential poisons and found nothing, that it is the object itself or rather the runes upon it that you believe to be the cause of his situation? You believe in *magic?*" Her mouth quirked at the corners. When Midnight did not answer, she replied with, "Interesting, very interesting."

"There are many strange and unexplainable things in this world, Miss Bird. Just because we do not understand or believe in them does not mean that they do not exist. Don't you agree?"

"More than you would think. Now, back to business. Do you have my notes on your cube?"

Midnight opened the desk drawer and pulled out a bundle of papers and handed them to Elldy.

"You insinuated a connection of some kind between these two artefacts, yes?"

Midnight nodded.

"We need to determine how a mask that was dug up in a

burial mound in Essex decades ago is connected to a cube in a locked box in an attic in London."

"I might be able to help with that," said a voice at the door.

"Giles?" Midnight was surprised by his old butler's sudden appearance. "You have seen this before, haven't you?" He held up the cube. "That is why you got upset earlier —because I had not informed you of my find?"

Giles Morgan sighed and looked at the floor. "Might I sit down, sir? My old bones are tired and secrets weigh heavily upon me."

Intrigued and a little disconcerted, Midnight indicated the Giles pull up a chair. "Does this have something to do with my father?"

"In a way, yes. But it is more connected to your mother. Although I have to confess that I do not know the whole story, and I admit that I am not sure where to start."

"The beginning would be nice," Midnight said brusquely.

Elldy interrupted. "Forgive me, but I feel I should like to visit the powder room. This is not something I need to be here for, I think."

"Do sit down, Miss Bird. I shall not reveal too much detail, but I do, however, believe that you may know some of the story already—judging by the notes you wrote on the cube."

"Am I the only person in the room who does not know what is going on here?" Midnight demanded. "Giles?"

"I am not one-hundred-percent sure, but I believe that cube belonged to your mother. And, Miss Bird, I am sure, can confirm this. The mask was donated to the museum by your father."

Stunned into momentary silence, Midnight looked from Giles to Elldy and back again.

Elldy cleared her throat. "I did know that the mask was donated by Josiah Gunn, yes. When you turned up at the museum asking for access to the storage basement, and then we discovered the open door, I did a little investigating of my own. That is why it took me a few days to come and see you; I wanted to be sure I was right. I had no clue that the mask was even missing until I came across your family's name in one of the archives. It was just a feeling, an instinct, if you will, that being as you are from a very wealthy background and you seemed so desperate to gain access to the archives, there might be some family connection between you and my museum.

"Once I found the document stating that Lord Gunn Senior had graciously given the museum the mask a long time before you were born, I assumed it might be that particular artefact you needed to see. And I went looking for it. Low and behold, it was not on the shelf where it should have been. Given what information I had already provided you with regarding your mysterious cube, I knew the two objects must be connected somehow."

"And just how did my father come to be in possession of the mask in the first place? Did it also belong to my mother?"

Giles answered Midnight's question. "He stole it."

"He what?" Midnight barked.

"Your father enjoyed attending archaeological digs when he first met your mother. They had not been acquainted for very long, but I could see that he was utterly smitten by her. I was not surprised; Josephine was a true beauty. There was something about your mother that enchanted anyone who encountered her. Your father was one of the many suitors who were vying for her attention.

"The story, as he told it to me, was that she would carry around that cube everywhere she went—almost like a talisman. Once, he asked her about it, and she told him that she was fascinated by Vikings and the old sagas of heroes and great beasts. The cube, she said, was her lucky charm, and it had obviously worked because she had met your father."

Giles paused to sigh before continuing his tale.

"Soon after, your father was called upon to sponsor the excavation of a proposed Viking burial mound in Essex. Of course, he could not resist the chance to impress his lovely Josephine and so, when the dig shut down for the day, your father went back… with me… and we dug a little further into the mound and—"

"Found the mask and stole it?" Elldy finished.

"Yes. That is the summary of what happened," Giles confirmed.

"It appears thievery is a family trait," she quipped.

"So why did he then donate the mask to the museum soon after he gave it to Mother? And why was her precious 'lucky charm' locked away in a box and left to gather dust in a corner of the attic?" Midnight asked.

"This is where my knowledge of the truth is a little lacking, I am afraid. Something happened, something bad enough to upset your mother so much that she refused to see your father anymore, at least until he had gotten rid of both the mask and the cube. I do not know exactly what, but I know it frightened both her and your father. Josiah told me to get rid of the cube and to never tell him what I had done with it as long as it was far away from the mask. That is when your father donated the mask to the museum."

"*You* hid the cube in the attic? Why did you not get rid of it like Father asked of you?"

"From what I had seen, it had seemed of such value and importance to Josephine that I could not imagine that she truly wanted to be rid of it. Some part of me had notions of pleasing her by gifting it back when she changed her mind." Giles smiled ruefully. "As I said, your mother had a strange effect on silly young men like myself. I never did tell your father what I had done with it, and he never asked me— neither did your mother... and then she died, and I forgot all about it until I saw you with it."

"That is why you were angry with me?"

"It was a shock, seeing the two artefacts together, and witnessing what they did."

"What did they do?" Elldy demanded, excitedly.

Midnight and Giles appeared not to hear her. "What else do you know, Giles? Anything that will help me free Arthur?

Giles shook his head. "That is all I know."

"Well, gentlemen. If I might make a suggestion? Given whatever happened to your parents when the artefacts were together, it would perhaps point to it happening again when they were in close proximity to each other at the museum. And whatever madness was caused, that is what affected the inspector. If that is true, then we just have to reverse whatever process started this whole mess."

Midnight stood and began pacing purposefully back and forth, deep in thought. "This feels wrong. Why would my mother keep something for so long, something that was obviously precious to her, and then just throw it away like it was nothing? She had that cube for years before she met my father. Even if the mask and cube together created a situation dire enough for Father to give the mask away, would Mother not have wanted to keep her 'good luck charm' knowing that, on its own, it held no danger for her?"

"That makes some sort of sense, I suppose. Perhaps she finally saw the cube for what it really was and knew she had to get rid of it?"

Elldy and Midnight both looked at Giles for the answer.

"No…" Giles said slowly. "No, I do not think that was the case. In truth, now I think about it, I must have known that she might want it back someday. That is why I chose to just hide it rather than throw it away. I truly believe it was still special to her. It was your father who was the most frightened. It was he who instructed me never to tell him what I had done with it."

"There has to be a way we can find out how these two artefacts are connected and what exactly happens when they are together," Midnight insisted.

"Perhaps we should go back to where it all started then— the burial mound where the mask was found. It is as good a place to begin as any, and I happen to know its location," said Elldy.

"You *have* been busy these last few days," Midnight said.

"It is my job, Lord Gunn. And my own personal policy: Never go anywhere or do anything without thorough preparation first. I am a woman in a man's world, I have to be better than them if I am to sit at the same table."

23

THE OTHERWORLD

JANUARY 26TH, 1863

Я|R

T he rocks that he lay upon dug into his flesh. They were not smooth with age but spiked and sharp and full of malevolence. The chain around his neck felt heavier with every day that passed. It burned his fur and bit into his skin with each slight movement of his head.

Shins was beaten and broken in ways he had not felt before. *She* had done this to him. She had been watching and waiting for his return, and now she had wreaked her revenge on him for his betrayal. An uncontrollable shiver coursed through his bruised body, causing him to whimper. She may yet forgive him. But it would not be for a very long time. He had committed the ultimate sin. He had lived with and protected a human—not just any human either but the one she wanted dead.

Shins drifted in and out of consciousness. Sometimes the pain was so bad that it roused him, and sometimes it caused him to lapse into blissful nothingness. He would have gladly preferred to remain in the latter state were it not for his need to escape and get back to Meriton House.

When her minions had captured and beaten him into

submission and he had been dragged before her, he had thought she would kill him. So notorious was her wrath that he had, at first, held no hope of survival. His broken body was physical proof of her anger, and yet she had held back. Perhaps she did harbour some long-lost feelings of affection for him after all.

Of course, he was glad to still be alive at the mercy of she who sat on the dragon-winged throne, but that did not help him. He must find a way to escape. The iron chains that bound him burned, made him weak, and prevented his bones from healing. He could not do this on his own.

Wrestling to stay awake, Shins could only think of one being who might be willing and able to help him: his one and only visitor, Tanaquill, who herself had been banished into eternal servitude and now brought him food and water each day.

In order to garner the fae's aid, he needed to flatter her into helping him, something that he had been working hard at since his imprisonment. Time was passing, and Tanaquill would be here soon to tend to him. He must be ready. He must stay awake.

The rattle of keys in the lock of his cell door alerted him. He waited until the fae was close enough to him that she could see his eyes reflecting the light of her torch, then he whimpered, wagging his tail most pathetically.

"Oh! My noble beast, you are pleased to see me," The fae stated in her musically seductive voice.

Shins wagged his tail harder, forcing himself to retain the whine that threatened to burst from his mouth. Tanaquill took off her tattered cloak and lay it on the hard ground beside him. She lay a hand upon his head and gently stroked him. He gave her his most adoring, pleading look and she could not resist.

"You and I are so very misused. *Her* jealousy cursed us both. I will unchain you once again so that you may soothe my injured soul with your words of adoration. Then, we will be free from the chains of melancholy for a few moments. You will be so grateful to have pleased me so," she crooned. Tanaquill rose and reached for a long piece of intricately carved wood that hung on the outer wall.

Shins felt instant relief as the chains that bound him fell away with each tap of the yew staff. He gave himself a moment to gather his thoughts and to focus what little remaining strength he had left, then, free from the iron that restricted his power, Shins the Barghest became Lord Rowland the man. There, on the black course rocks, naked and bruised, Rowland lifted his stiff, aching body to a seated position, raised his head and fixed the fae with the brightest smile he could muster.

"Thank you, my lady, all powerful and most gracious Gloriana," he cooed.

Tanaquill beamed at him, a prideful excitement exploded in her eyes. "Yes! Yes, indeed, my most adoring one. Tell me again of my stolen past. Tell me how it was *I* whom the poet Edmund did lament. Tell it true that all should hear of how *she* robbed me of my glorious Gloriana."

"Warm me first, my Leanan Sídhe? If I am to do justice to your greatness, I cannot do so with this chill in my poor bones. I must be allowed to bathe in your glow for I am the only one who can sing your song of truth," Rowland pleaded.

Tanaquill gave him her tattered cloak, which he wrapped around his shoulders, relived at even this minimal comfort.

"Speak on, Lord Rowland, for I am impatient to hear your gratitudes."

Rowland smiled. This malignant phantom's conceit was

her downfall. He cleared his throat and began to recite the epic poem, "The Faerie Queene" by Edmund Spencer.

"Upon a great adventure he was bond,
That greatest Gloriana to him gave,
That greatest Glorious Queene of Faerie lond,
To winne him worship, and her grace to have,
Which of all earthly things he most did crave..."
Rowland continued on with his impassioned performance
whilst Tanaquill revelled in her own self-importance.
"...So pure an innocent, as that same lambe,
She was in life and every vertuous lore,
And by descent from Royall lynage came
Of ancient Kings and Queenes, that had of yore
Their scepters stretcht from East to Westerne shore,
And all the world in their subjection held;
Till that infernall feend with foule uprore
Forwasted all their land, and them expeld:
Whom to avenge, she had this Knight from far compeld."

By the time Rowland had reached the end of the first canto, his throat became dry and his voice hoarse. He paused to cough.

"My lord, my knight, why have you stopped?" Tanaquill demanded. "I am only just beginning to dispatch of this cursed melancholia."

"I am thirsty, your gloriousness. Grant me pity and give me water?"

Tanaquill reached for the flagon of water and poured him a bowlful. Still full of egocentric pride, she continued to lament her sorrowful tale of injustice. "It pains me to think that *she* takes credit for this masterpiece when it was my own perfection that served as his muse. And then I must suffer further insult when he did dedicate his poem to his own queen of Middle Earth, *Elizabeth!*" she spat. "Years and years I did inspire his song and all were to know of the great and beautiful Tanaquill. And then it was *her* jealousy that did provoke my cursed soul. Ohhh! Am I to be banished and forgotten for an eternity? Is her light so dim that she cannot tolerate the shine of another?"

Rowland seized his chance. Placing the bowl on the floor, he shuffled forward and took both of Tanaquill's hands in his own.

"Beautiful Leanan Sídhe, if I were free to roam Middle Earth once more, I would stop at nothing to restore your name to all its shining glory. All of the realms would know of the majesty of the Lady Tanaquill, the muse of poets and inspirer of creativity. I could right this wrong you have been forced to endure these last centuries, and she would be forced to recognise your truth."

Tanaquill stroked his face. "Of course you would, my lord. I am more than worthy of your love and loyalty. However, I fear that even with you by my side, we would not succeed in this endeavour. She is too powerful now. She presents herself only as air and darkness upon the dragon-winged throne. With no physical body, none can harm her, and therefore, I must suffer this injustice for an eternity, like the proverbial princess in the tower, awaiting her knight—a knight that will never come for none are formidable as she."

"I know of one. Free me, and I shall bring him here to free you, that I promise," Rowland implored.

"You do? Who is this powerful knight?" Tanaquill demanded eagerly

"Not a knight, my lady, a prince! He is the man I have served in Middle Earth and the reason I am enchained in here." Improvising now, Rowland laid down his plan. "So intimidated is she by him that she has forbidden me to return to him would that I reveal her secrets and she garner his wrath. I beg of you, oh beautiful lady, grant me freedom from this realm, help me to return to him, and I will bring you the key to your redemption."

Tanaquill was won over; the notion of her return to glory was too great an opportunity to pass by. She stood and flounced regally to the door of his cell and held it open.

"Take this blackthorn staff," she instructed, handing him the carved piece that she had used to release his chains. "Run forth and find your prince and fetch him here to fight for me. I shall prepare for your return, Lord Rowland. It is time for Lady Tanaquill to rise again."

24

THE SAFFRON WALDEN MOUND
JANUARY 26TH 1863

ЯⅡR

A chill mist clung to the late evening/early morning air, making the trees in the forest just outside of the small market town of Saffron Walden in Essex appear to be floating in a sea of grey soup. It was the kind of night where all sound was swallowed by the wall of mist and leafless sentries that surrounded the small field in which the barrow stood, domed and unassuming.

Midnight, Giles and Elldy stood beside the earthy hump with a caved-in top that indicated that this grave site had been previously robbed—quite literally in the instance of the mask —by a long-gone team of archaeologists. Dead nettles, tangled weeds, and other scrubland detritus were strewn about its surface, which had lain undisturbed since its well-intentioned defilement.

"According to the records, the grave dates back to around the ninth or tenth century," Elldy told them. "The skeletal remains of a large male were discovered as well as a number of grave goods, including a sword, an amber necklace, a bejewelled knife, six arrow heads, and a ring-headed pin. And there's the mask... but of course no one, aside from Josiah Gunn, knew of it at the time," she added.

"What happens now?" Giles asked.

"I suppose we get the objects together and see what happens," Midnight replied.

Giles opened the burlap sack he was carrying and extracted the already glowing mask. He wore leather gloves so as not to let his skin come into contact with it. Laying the sack on the damp grass, Giles carefully placed the mask on top of it, face-side up.

Midnight then reached into his deep coat pocket and pulled out his cube. It too was glowing. Removing his own gloves, Midnight held the cube aloft and focused his energy. The same shining runic symbols he had seen at home in his study emanated an almost blinding light as the corner sections of the cube popped open. Midnight channelled more energy into the object, and then, the mask began its spinning arial display once again. He heard Elldy gasp in awe and surprise, as the cube shone brighter and brighter and the mask spun faster and faster until the very ground beneath their feet shook.

"Look!" Elldy cried, and pointed to the east side of the barrow where they stood.

The grass and earth of the mound began to ripple and move, eventually falling away to reveal a large dark opening from which a horrifying ghostly green and ravaged figure emerged. The thing was clothed in ragged breeches and tunic, with a belt at its waist from which hung a grand sword and a mighty axe. Bits of shrivelled flesh, bone and sinew were visible through the rips in the fabric. Strands of long, plaited hair clung perilously to the withered skin of its scalp. It raised its mangled head as if sniffing the air then fixed its milky dead eyes on Midnight. As soon as the entity identified its target, it roared fiercely. The mask stopped spinning and fell to the ground, still glowing. A thin, bright tendril of light streamed from it straight towards the ghastly apparition. The entity inhaled the light deeply, and as it did so, its form liquified and morphed into something all-too-familiar- mac and bowler hat perfectly in situ.

"Inspector Gredge!" Giles shouted, taken aback.

"No. It is not," said Midnight.

Despite looking exactly like Arthur Gredge, this thing was a frighteningly brilliant copy of him. Its greenish glow had disappeared, and it had, for all intents and purposes, taken on the identity of the mask's last wearer.

"It is a doppelgänger! This explains everything! Arthur is not possessed. He is not a killer. This thing is connected to him through the mask. That is why Arthur's memories appeared so odd to me," Midnight declared with an overwhelming sense of relief. "Because they were not entirely his!"

"All well and good," Elly yelled. "But how do you prove that in a court? And what is more, how do you get rid of it? It looks very angry!"

"I have absolutely no clue!" Midnight shouted over the creature's roar. "I suggest we figure out a strategy soon though." Midnight considered blasting it with his dark power but did not yet understand how or if it might affect the real Gredge; he quickly surmised that any damage the creature may suffer, could perhaps rebound upon his friend. The creature had seemingly already penetrated Gredge's mind, could Midnight risk a full-on attack?

The three of them backed slowly away as the anger-fuelled creature advanced menacingly towards them, its arms outstretched like double bayonets.

"Sir!" Giles cried out a warning as the thing lunged

towards his master. The old butler pulled out his pistol and shot,

"No!" Midnight cried but the bullet went straight through the Gredge-creature, hitting the mound instead.

Elldy stumbled backwards, tripping over the mask on the ground. Landing on her rear, the mask close by, Elldy had an idea; picking up a large rock she slammed it down on the artefact. The doppelgänger's head swung around to look directly at her, and it roared furiously, running towards her. Elldy picked herself up and ran, grateful to be wearing breeches and not cumbersome flounces of skirt.

"Hey! Hey! Over here, you scurrilous rat," Midnight shouted as he poured more energy into the cube, hoping that it would magnify his powers the same as his selenite pendant did, whilst wishing he'd had the foresight to wear it tonight.

The cube now vibrated and throbbed violently in his hand. He could feel parts of it moving beneath his fingers as if it were made of liquid and not wood and silver. Was this the key to stopping the creature? With a sudden shift in the atmosphere, a growing sphere of blue light appeared between him and the undead creature. Midnight frowned at the sphere's familiarity; it was the same as the portal he had seen at the stone circle in Scotland. The one that Shins had—

"Shins?" he cried as a vast hairy bulk emerged from the sphere and launched himself at the oncoming threat.

Shins bounced off the Gredge-replicant's chest, sending it toppling to the ground. As the creature flailed around, trying to right itself, Shins made a dash for the mask. He scooped it up in his massive jaw and ran for the black hole in the mound.

Shins disappeared into the belly of the barrow with the enraged doppelgänger following, leaving Giles, Elldy, and Midnight at a loss as to what to do next. They did not have long to ponder, as a few seconds later, Shins came bounding out again sans mask and with no sign of the undead Viking.

"Shins! What happened to you? I have been so worried. What have you done with the mask?" Midnight had so many questions he needed answers to, but the mutt did not pause to reunite. Everything was happening at lightning pace.

He ran straight at Midnight and clamped his teeth around the wrist of the hand that still held the pulsating cube, causing Midnight to howl in pain and promptly drop it. As soon as the cube left his hand, it returned to its previous inanimate form.

The blue portal vanished instantly, there was a rumbling of earth as the Draugr door in the mound resealed itself, leaving no trace it had ever been there. All was silent aside from the panicked panting of Widdershins. Streams of billowing breath drifted from his gaping maw, he staggered to one side then collapsed in a shuddering heap on the ground and did not move.

25

MERITON HOUSE

THE MORNING OF JANUARY 27TH 1863

ℜℜ

Polly had not stopped crying all morning, first with relief at Shins' return, then with grief at the extent of his injuries. Giles and Midnight had carried his bulk from the carriage, up the front steps, and through to the parlour just before sunrise, and had lain the great beast beside the roaring fire. Using the light from the flames, Midnight had channelled warm, healing energy to soothe and heal Shins to full health. And now, Polly had her little arms wrapped around his wide neck, her wet cheeks buried in his bushy, dishevelled fur whilst Shins panted contentedly, wagging his tail, and giving Polly the occasional reassuring chuff.

Mrs Phillips had brought the cold and exhausted group bowls of steaming hot porridge with honey and a large pot of freshly brewed, strong tea. Once everyone had settled and Midnight had recounted the events to a very insistent Polly, they began to dissect and discuss what had transpired at Saffron Walden Barrow.

"But what exactly is a Draugr, Papa, and why was it dressed up like the inspector and killing people?" Polly asked.

Both Midnight and Elldy had brought many books down from the library and had busied themselves in their continued research of Norse mythology. Midnight read a passage from the book he was holding so Polly and the rest of the gathered group could hear.

"It says here that Draugr, translated, means after-walker or a spirit that walks after death."

"Like a ghost?" Polly gasped.

"Not quite but very similar, I think. A Draugr is a jealous, restless spirit of a Viking warrior. They live in their burial mounds, guarding their treasures. However, unlike ghosts, Draugrs have corporeal bodies that can shapeshift into any form," Midnight read.

"What would a Draugr be jealous of exactly?" Polly wondered.

"The living, I suspect. The book states that once awoken, the enraged Draugr takes on the appearance of the first person it touches and subsequently takes the life essence of those its host comes into physical contact with. That is what helps it to sustain its corporeal form."

"This puts me in mind of some other legends of old," Elldy pondered. "The Draugr followed the mask back into its grave. It seems that replacing the stolen object is all that was needed to send it back to where it came from. But then why has it taken this long for the Draugr to emerge? Why did it not embark on a killing spree decades ago when its grave was first disturbed, and the treasure taken?" She wondered.

The group fell silent for a moment while they thought this through. Nobody could say for sure why events had unfolded as they had. Then, Midnight offered his suggestion.

"It must have something to do with my cube, although I do not see how since it belonged to Mother before she even met Father. The mask reacted to the cube when they were in close proximity, almost as if it triggered something. That day at the museum, when I first came to visit you, Miss Bird. That was the day that Arthur found the mask and tried it on. Could it be that the Draugr spirit was attached to the artefact, imbued with it? And that the cube acted as a key to releasing it fully into the realm of the living? It took on Gredge's appearance so that would make sense as he would be the first person to touch the mask after the cube had activated it. Giles, Miss Bird, what do you think?"

"Sounds plausible," Giles agreed with a shrug.

"I read somewhere that heavy stones were laid atop the graves of witches to prevent them from rising after death to wreak revenge on those who had killed them. One can find similar stories in Europe of suspected vampires being buried face down, decapitated and their mouths filled with stones to prevent them from walking after death. The mask may have served the same purpose."

Polly gasped again, louder this time, and Midnight frowned.

"Of all the things in this world and the next, vampires are not real, sweetheart," Midnight said reassuringly.

"Ohhh! But I wish they was, Papa!" Her cockney accent seeped through. "Imagine that!" Polly squealed; eyes bright with excitement.

"Polly Gunn, you are without a doubt the single most unpredictable child I have ever met." Midnight smiled and shook his head in mirth. "I think it is time for you to go and get washed and dressed. Miss Carmichael will be awake soon, and there is no excuse for missing your lessons today."

"But—" Polly protested.

"Goat's butt," Mrs Phillips interrupted. "Do as your father says and be off with you now. Come on, help me take the breakfast pots away."

"Isn't that Laura's job?" Polly said sulkily.

"Laura is not yet up. Now mind your tongue or the Devil shall bite it off," Mrs Phillips chided, and the pair of them gathered up the crockery and left, Polly still muttering her protests at missing all of the drama.

"She is a handful," Elldy declared.

"That she is," Midnight agreed. "Now, you were saying, Miss Bird?"

"Yes, thank you. I was referring to the various methods in folklore of ensuring the dead stay dead. If the mask was the key to the Draugr's eternal incarceration, and the cube acted as a key to unlocking it, it must be connected. There can be no doubt. Mr Morgan," she addressed Giles, "are you sure you can recall nothing else about Mrs Gunn's precious cube? Anything at all that might help us understand its origin?"

"Nothing, I am afraid. Miss Josephine did not talk of her past or her family, at least not in my presence. Master Josiah would be the one to ask if he were here, he and she were inseparable."

"Thank you, Giles. I only wish I had known about the cube sooner. I do not blame you. Fear not," Midnight said as Giles began to protest. "It matters not now. I am not convinced that knowing where my mother obtained the artefact will help us vindicate Arthur anyway."

Midnight turned to Shins. "I must thank you for saving us tonight. I know I have already asked you, but I wonder if you might tell me how you found us. We do not need Polly to translate if you would let me see," Midnight asked, referring to Shins allowing him to see his thoughts.

Shins whined and shook his head. Midnight sighed, there was no forcing the mutt into an explanation right now, especially after what the poor creature had endured judging by the extent of the injuries Midnight had healed. However, he needed to let Shins know that this was a matter that must be discussed at some point. Midnight had many burning questions pertaining to the Other, and he had a distinct feeling that Shins was hiding something.

"I see. Well then, I suppose I must respect your wishes… for now," Midnight added. He addressed the rest of the group, "That only leaves us with the very great and difficult task of proving Arthur's innocence, without us all being declared insane and committed to the asylum. Does anyone have any thoughts?"

26

STONES END
JANUARY 27TH 1863

ЯⵏR

"I know what I saw, Superintendent Branford. I am an upstanding and law-abiding member of society." Miss Elldy Bird sat even straighter in her seat as she spoke.

"That is all well and good, madame. However, it does not aid me in any way in releasing Arthur Gredge. I cannot go to a judge with fanciful tales of doppelgängers or long-lost revengeful twin brothers. It is ridiculous! The courts need evidence, irrefutable proof that Gredge did not commit those murders. I have his confession, witness statements. You have offered me nothing substantial at all."

"Good sir, if I may cut in?" Midnight did so anyway without waiting for Branford's permission. "You know that I have worked with Scotland Yard for quite some years now. I have never given you or the commissioner any cause to doubt my word. I would be inclined to question the validity of a confession from a man who is clearly suffering from a malady of the mind. I must take some responsibility for the inspector's current state. The attack on my person and the subsequent statements of my maid and young daughter appeared to seal his fate, but we know that cannot be the truth. *You* know it cannot be the truth. I give you my word now, as a gentleman, that Miss Bird is telling the truth. *Someone* out there is impersonating Arthur Gredge! For what reason, we do not know but our consciences cannot allow this case to go to trial."

Branford considered their pleas for a moment, his fingers tapping out rhythmically on his desktop. Finally, he let out a heavy sigh. "I have to admit that I have struggled with the idea of Gredge being capable of cold-blooded murder. And I must agree that his mind is not as it should be, and as Sergeant Rowe has reported to me, Gredge has been displaying some very worrying behaviour these last months. There is sense in your argument, and I am inclined to agree with you regarding his confession. He still maintains that he cannot recall a thing about the incidents in question. But I do not feel that a judge would release him on gut feeling alone."

"Then what else can we do? There must be something, some way of preventing him from being tried for three murders he did not commit," Midnight insisted.

"I can think of only one way that Gredge might be spared the hangman's noose, but I am not sure it is a fate as merciful as a quick death." Branford said.

Midnight frowned. "Exactly what are you proposing?"

"He agrees to sign over power of attorney to you, and you have him committed to the asylum for rehabilitation. You would need to declare yourself his sponsor and sign a legal document that says you agree to ensure his continued care and treatment during the ongoing investigation. He would also need to resign from the force. There is, at present, no way of clearing him of these charges. If the case goes to trial as it is, Arthur will hang. However, this way, it gives us time to continue the investigation and find this deplorable doppelgänger you both insist is the real culprit."

"That is absurd!" Elly protested, knowing full well that they would never be able to find and arrest anyone.

"I will do it," Midnight said at the same time.

Elldy looked at Midnight with incredulity. "You would allow this injustice? I thought you said the man was your friend?"

"It is as Superintendent Branford says. At this moment in time, there is no other feasible way of saving Gredge from the gallows. I will do it. I will do whatever it takes to save my friend from harm."

Outside of the building at Stone's End, Elldy rounded on Midnight. "How could you? All of that effort we have gone through to have him released, and now you are taking over his entire life and shoving him in the lunatic asylum! Why?"

"Calm yourself, Miss Bird. Things are not as they seem. There is more than one way to skin a cat." Midnight winked and grinned at her.

"What are you planning, sir?"

"Oh, nothing. Absolutely nothing at all."

27

SOUTHWARK MAGISTRATES COURT
FEBRUARY 1ST 1863

ЯⱵR

"**M**otion carried!" the judge declared and banged his gavel once on the wooden block to his right. "It is this court's decision that Mr Arthur Gredge of Little Surrey Street, London is to be taken henceforth until such a time as he is capable of standing trial, or new evidence is presented in court, and with immediate effect, to the asylum, as recommended by the medical team, where he will remain for continuous assessment and rehabilitation. Court dismissed."

"Murderer! You'll not get away with this!" a man shouted from the public gallery, shaking his fist at Gredge as he was led by Sergeant Rowe from the dock.

Gredge kept his eyes lowered and looked truly upset as he shuffled away. In the corridor that led to the street, Rowe paused and held out a rough-looking sack.

"Best put this on, boss. There's a crowd outside, and they ain't in the best of moods."

Gredge made no protest and allowed Rowe to cover his head with the sack.

"This way, boss. The prison cart is waiting outside. Won't

be long, and you can settle in, take some time out, and they will look after you."

The noise of an angry mob grew louder as they neared the exit, and Gredge prepared himself for what was to come. A chill blast of air caught him by surprise as Rowe pushed open the door. He gasped then yelped as something hard hit him in the chest and fell to the floor with a thud. More missiles were thrown, most of which missed their target, or hit Rowe, but it was the insults that hurt Arthur the most.

"Piece of shite copper!" one man shouted.

"Hang 'im, the child-molesting bastard!" a female voice cried.

"Snap his worthless neck!" said another.

He could not see much through the coarse burlap threads, but he could sense there was a fair crowd and they were beginning to close in on him. Rowe and another police officer were doing their best to push the hecklers back, but Gredge was now being punched and kicked by many hands and feet as they struggled through the mob.

"Benny! Keep the bleeders off, will you? Watch them lot there!" Rowe shouted his orders at the young constable. "Come on, boss. This way."

Gredge could not tell what was happening now. Rowe suddenly pushed down on his head, causing him to almost bend in half. He was surrounded by so many bodies he did not know which way to go. Then Rowe was bent over him and whispering something in his ear, but he couldn't make it out over the ruckus. Light made him squint as the sack was pulled from his head and replaced by a tweed cap, and a large, knitted scarf was flung around his neck. At the same time a heavy coat settled around his shoulders. Rowe's hand was gone from his arm, and Gredge was frightened and confused. He glanced up a little and saw the open door of an unmarked black carriage before him. A hand reached out to him, and instinctively he took it. Someone heaved him inside, the door slammed, and he heard the driver yell.

"Hah!"

The carriage lurched forward and moved away from the baying mob. He could hear the fading police whistles grow quiet as the carriage carried him further. It was then that he realised he lay in a heap on the floor of the moving vehicle. He felt a hand on his shoulder then and a gentle, familiar voice spoke.

"You can get up now, Arthur. You are free."

"Midnight? That you? What—what are you doing here? This isn't the cart. What's going on?" Arthur scrambled up on to the seat opposite his friend and stared in amazement. He was not, as he had correctly determined, in the rickety old prison cart but in a small black carriage with blinds at the windows that blocked out most of the light.

"It is good to see you again, my friend," Midnight said with genuine affection. "You have probably gathered that you are not on your way to the asylum and that you have, in fact, escaped that fate."

"You stupid sod! Don't you know what you've done?"

"Not quite the reaction I was expecting, Arthur," Midnight confessed.

"When I don't turn up, where the bleedin' Hell do you think they are going to look first? You are in charge of my estate, you fool. Meriton is the first place they will go! At this rate, you'll have us both hanging from a rope."

"Arthur, do you really believe me so incapable of plotting this great escape that I would not have thought of every contingency first? Give me a little credit, please. Now, are you going to let me explain, or are you going to call me names again?"

"Explain then, and it had better be good."

"I am prepared to overlook your ungrateful continuance on account of what you have suffered. Now, where was I? Ah, yes. As I was saying, you are not en route to the asylum. However, another Arthur Gredge is." He held up his hand to shush Gredge. "Do let me finish? Part of the agreement I made with Branford was that I be permitted to select which hospital you were to go to and which medical team were to assess you. It just so happens, that with fortunate coincidence, the wing for maladies of the mind at Saint Francis—yes, the Saint Francis that I own—has opened early and the very agreeable Nurse Carstairs and her team have been assigned to care for you—I mean, my Arthur—for the foreseeable future. I am, as you know, not in favour of such treatments and practices for mental illnesses as are other asylums, which means Arthur will not be suffering electric shocks or having to be force fed etcetera. He will be enjoying a private room with three square meals a day, walks in the garden, regular bathing, clean clothes, and a safe warm bed to sleep in every night as well as a small retainer for keeping his mouth shut until we can figure out a long-term solution for this mess."

Gredge looked more confused than ever.

"What do you mean 'another Arthur'? And where the bleedin' Hell am I supposed to go? Who am I meant to be?"

"No need to fret. My Arthur is someone I am acquainted with from the rookery who needs to lay low for a while. His usual abode is somewhat unavailable, shall we say, and so, he was more than happy to do this little favour for me. As for you, my friend. You will have to live in my basement for a few days until I can safely transfer you into the care of Miss Bird. I am afraid there is a watcher outside Meriton and has been for some time. I do not think Branford completely trusts me. Imagine that? Incidentally, if you would be kind enough to allow me to smuggle you into Meriton via the back entrance, that would save me a lot of trouble."

"Madness! Utter madness, Midnight. You really think this will work?" Gredge said.

"It has to. It is the only plan any of us could put together in such a short time. I have arranged for a Doctor of Psychology to visit with you to help get your thoughts in order, as well as a few other methods if you are willing to try. I am responsible for this, Arthur, and I am profoundly sorry for your suffering over the years. Please, allow me to help you and put things right?"

"Looks like I don't have much of a choice," Gredge huffed.

"No, I suppose not."

"Why is the museum woman involved in all of this anyway? Struck me as a bit of a battle axe, she did."

"There is much to explain, Arthur. We will be at Meriton very soon, and then, I will tell you everything. My daughter is very excited to have you as our guest, by the way."

"I missed her birthday," Gredge said miserably.

"That you did. But there is plenty of time to make up for that. And Arthur?"

"Hmm?"

"Do not ever think that you are not welcome in my house."

28

MERITON
FEBRUARY 14TH 1863

$\mathcal{R}\|\mathsf{R}$

"Enter," Midnight said to the knock on his study door. A moment later, a very upset Agnes Carmichael walked in carrying a letter.

"Pardon the intrusion, Lord Gunn. I know you are busy, but I wish to speak to you about a personal matter." This last word she choked out and tears spilled down her cheeks.

Midnight immediately rose from his chair and went to her to guide her to another. "Sit down, Miss Carmichael. Whatever is the matter?" He spotted the letter in her trembling hands. "Is that news from home?"

Agnes nodded and he feared the worse.

"Your brother?"

"Yes," she sobbed. "Father writes that he is dead. Oh, but it is horrible." Fat tears plopped onto the paper, causing some of the inked words to run.

"I am truly sorry for your loss. You will, of course, need some time off to grieve."

"Thank you, sir. But it is not for that reason that I come to you now. I need to go home, to America."

"I see. I am happy to let you go, of course, but the war—the shipping blockades? Not to mention the risk to you travelling without a chaperone. Should anything happen to you during your travels, I would never forgive myself." *Not to mention that Polly would crucify me,* he thought.

"I had not thought. Oh, but I must go. It is so terrible. Mother and Father cannot deal with this alone."

"Is there no other family out there who could assist them with the arrangements?" asked Midnight.

"No. You do not understand. Here. Read this." Agnes pushed the letter towards him.

He took it from her and began to skim over the words on the paper.

Dearest, darling Agnes,

It pains me greatly to have to inform you that your brother is dead. We received a telegram not a week ago from his commanding officer informing us of the terrible news.

We, of course, immediately wrote back asking for his body to be brought home to us so that we may provide him with a decent burial as is proper, but we were refused our request. Your mother is beside herself with grief. As am I, dear one. I have since written many letters and telegrams to make enquiries of the whereabouts of your brother's body and to attempt to find out why we are continuously denied the right to bury him at home to no avail.

This past week, rumours of something terrible happening to our soldiers are circulating in the press. There is much revolt amongst the troops with many deserting and telling frightening tales of men going missing in their battalions only to be discovered days later in a mutilated state. I can only assume our boy to be one of them, and therefore they will not allow us to see him. I fear he is destined to be buried in a pit with no marker and no one to grieve over his grave.

Mother and I cannot bear it any longer. Our hearts are broken, and we wish you were home with us to offer us comfort, but alas, that cannot be. It is not safe for you here. War is no place for you, my darling daughter. Please write back when you receive this letter and let us know you are safe and well.

All my love,

Father

Midnight finished reading and handed the letter back to Agnes, who was utterly inconsolable. He could not find the words to comfort her, so he did the only thing he could think of and poured her a large glass of brandy.

"Drink this. It will help," he said as he handed her the glass.

She gulped it down in two swallows, which made her cough. When she recovered, she said,

"You see now why I must go home. Father says not to go, but I can tell he needs me there. I need to help him find out what happened to my brother. Sir, please?" she begged.

"You will go home, and I will accompany you. I will not see you travel alone in these dangerous times. Leave everything to me. I will make all of the necessary arrangements so all you need do is write back to your father and tell him to expect us."

Agnes sobbed even louder and flung her arms around him in gratitude. At the same time, Laura entered the room to stoke the fire. She started at the sight of Agnes draped all over her master, crying like an infant.

"Begging your pardon," Laura said as she bobbed a curtsey and backed out of the room, her cheeks aflame.

Midnight spotted her and called her back. "Miss Carter. Miss Carmichael has had bad news from home, and I need to make travel arrangements to America as soon as possible. Please find Giles and ask him to come to my study."

"Yes, sir," Laura said quietly. 'Bad news from home' could mean only one thing: the death of her brother. Laura hurried away from the study to find Giles, cheeks still blazing but with shame this time.

Giles entered a few minutes later, and Midnight set about organising travel arrangements with him. Agnes went gratefully back to her room to write back to her family while Giles curated a list of tasks and errands for Laura and Charlie to run.

"I need to organise this as soon as possible, Giles. There is no telling how long it will take for us to reach America given the state of things there. I do not even know if we will be allowed through the shipping blockades, but I must at least try. It is the right thing to do."

"Of course, sir. You can count on us to run the house while you are away, naturally."

"I know." Midnight put his hand on Giles shoulder and gave it a friendly squeeze. "I am more than blessed. Be sure to keep an eye on my daughter, too. Do not let her run you all ragged," he jested. "I will leave you to it, then, for the time being. I must visit Arthur at Crawley Manor in the coming days, and ensure his doctor's fees are paid up well in advance whilst I am away." He heard running footsteps outside the room, then Polly entered looking most perturbed.

"What is wrong with everyone today? Aggie's locked herself in her room, and Laura's got a face like bleedin' thunder! I've been making cards all mornin' and no one wants one." She sulked.

"Cards?" Midnight asked.

Polly held up a fistful of hearts that she had cut out and painted red with little bits of white lacey ribbon attached to the bottom of each one. "Happy Valentine's Day, Papa!"

29

CRAWLEY MANOR
FEBRUARY 27TH 1863

Я║Я

"He needs more time. The doctor says he is recovering well, but he has a long way to go before his mind is well again."

"That is good to hear, Miss Bird. I should like to visit with him now if I may?" Midnight made to step around his host, assuming she would follow him upstairs to the room in which Arthur had been encamped the last ten days.

Elldy put out her arm to stop him passing. "I am afraid Mr Gredge is not allowed any visitors at this time," she said.

Midnight tilted his head. "Oh? And why is that and on whose orders, may I ask?" he sounded concerned.

"The doctor believes he needs rest, and peace and quiet to aid his recovery with *no* disturbances," she added.

"I see," Midnight said. "Well, in that case—" He held out his hand to her, and she reciprocated by placing hers in his. Midnight smiled ruefully. "You are lying, Miss Bird." He gripped her hand tighter, preventing her from pulling away. "And I want to know why."

"Sir! Let go of me this instant or I shall scream!" Elldy glared at him whilst attempting to free herself from his grip.

"Scream all you like, madame, but I will see my friend *now,* and you had better wish that he is safe and well." He let go of her hand and strode purposefully towards the staircase.

"No! I will not allow this intrusion. This is my home and—"

"And Arthur is my friend."

Midnight took the stairs two at a time and reached the door to Arthur's room within moments. Not even bothering to knock, he barged into the room. It was empty. The bed was made, the room was clean, not one sign that Arthur Gredge had ever been there remained.

Midnight swung around to face Elldy, who looked worried. "Explain."

"He left."

"When? Why?"

"Three days ago. He left a note for you but asked me not to give it to you for seven days."

"Miss Bird, give me the note."

Elldy sighed. "Wait here. I will go and fetch it."

While she was gone, Midnight searched the room, pulling out drawers and riffling through them, checking under the mattress for anything Gredge may have left behind. He even pulled back the rug but found nothing. Midnight cursed and ran his hand through his hair.

"I can assure you that your friend is not hiding under the rug, Lord Gunn." Striding forwards into the room, Elldy handed him the letter from Gredge. He took it from her and went to stand by the window to read it. He recognised Arthur's familiar scrawl at once, the letter was no forgery.

Midnight,

I had to go. This is not who I am, this quivering, confused wreck of a man. Do not blame yourself for my troubles; you are not responsible for me. I got myself into this, and I will get myself out.

Don't blame Miss Bird for not telling you about my plan either. She was not aware of it until I was practically out of the door. She is a good woman. Be kind to her as she has been kind to me.

I will contact you further when I am ready. Since you are my power of attorney now, I would ask a small favour; Miss Bird has loaned me some money to see me through, and I would appreciate it if you would repay her from my own bank account as I do not have access to it at present.

Please, do not come looking for me. I ask as your friend, let me do this alone.

Regards,

Arthur

Midnight lowered the hand that held Gredge's goodbye and stared out of the window. Everything he and Arthur had been through together, and this is how he chose to leave things?

"I am sorry I did not bring you the letter sooner, Lord Gunn, but he made me promise. He said he needed time to plan so that you could not find him. He was of the opinion you would ignore his request not to look for him," Elldy said.

"Ahhh." Midnight shook his head and sighed. "He would be correct in that assumption. Miss Bird, you must have spoken to him before he left, you must know more than you are telling me," he said, making no attempt to disguise the pleading tone in his voice.

"What is written in his letter is much the same as what he told me, I am afraid. I think the Inspector is used to being in control of himself and his life. He seems to be the type of man whose career meant everything to him, and he took pride in his work."

"He was a damn good police officer, indeed," Midnight agreed. "I can see how Arthur would be upset about losing his position. But if he could have just waited a while until we could work out a way of proving him innocent—"

"I do not think Mr Gredge was willing to take that risk. His mind is unsettled. He felt weakened and vulnerable. I think he wanted to go away for a while and clear his head. At least, then, he would have the strength to continue to fight his own fight upon his return," Elldy reasoned.

"If he returns," Midnight replied. "Send a note to my bank with the amount Arthur owes you. I will leave you the details, and I will organise a payment to you as soon as possible. It is the least I can do. It is what he has asked of me." Midnight put the letter in his pocket and turned to leave.

Elldy followed him down the stairs. They shook hands at the front entrance.

"I apologise if I have hurt or offended you in any way, Miss Bird. I am afraid I am rather protective of my friends. I do not have that many you see. I am grateful for your part in this whole affair and for your care of Arthur. I will be in touch when I return from America."

"America?" Elldy said, taken aback.

"Yes. I have urgent business there. I sail in a few days. Do not worry. I will ensure you have your payment before I leave. Good day to you, Miss Bird."

"Good day, Lord Gunn."

30

MERITON

MARCH 1ST 1863

ЯⱤ

T he only light in the parlour came from the fire that flickered and spat accusingly at Midnight. He wanted the darkness to swallow him whole and dull the pain of failure. He had let Arthur down, and now his only friend in the world was gone, possibly for good. The Gunn household had been a woeful, subdued mess the last few days, and now, he sat here alone, facing a long and desolate journey across a vast ocean. He had no idea what he would experience along the way or what he might eventually come home to. How had it all gone so horribly wrong? Mentally, he ticked off the list of emotional blows of the last week.

Arthur had run away to Lord knew where with no inkling as to when or if he might return. Branford had people watching his every move, a nugget of information that had come from Sergeant Rowe who had told Midnight that the super had it in mind to meticulously go over the details of every case that he and Arthur had ever worked on together. According to Rowe, Branford blamed Midnight for the loss of his best detective and was determined to find some dirt on him as recompense.

Polly was not speaking to him since she had discovered that he was escorting her governess back to America, with no immediate date for their return as yet.

But one of the worst hits had come as a shock to the entire household. Miss Carter had handed in her resignation. Of course, Polly blamed him for this as well, and as fat tears of grief had run rivers down her plump cheeks, she had accused him of being as 'blind and as daft as a one-winged bat in a bakery'. Those were the last words she had spoken to him in a whole forty-eight hours. He had desperately wanted to talk to Laura alone, but with the rush of his last-minute travel plans, the packing, and everything else that the universe had thrown his way lately, he had not found an opportune moment before she had left early one morning whilst the rest of the household still slept.

The cut crystal glass in his hand sparkled in the light of the flames causing the deep amber liquid inside to shine alluringly. He lifted the receptacle to his mouth and gulped down the contents in one swallow, hoping that the heat of the warmed brandy would dull the ache in his heart. It did not, and so, he poured himself another, and drank it down—and another. He kept going until the bottle was two-thirds empty, and at last, he welcomed the dizzy distance of drunkenness.

Sometime later, when the heat of the fire had died and the chill air stirred him from his blissful oblivion, Midnight felt a hand on his shoulder. It was Giles, and although he stood there clothed in his night wear, monogrammed robe and slippers, he did not look as though he had slept at all.

"May I sit a while, sir?"

"Of course, Giles." Midnight slurred, still heavy with alcohol-induced sleep.

Midnight pushed himself back from his slumped position to sit upright in his chair. He did not ask but poured his old butler a generous measure of the brandy and offered it to him. Giles took it gratefully, raised his glass in a silent toast, and sipped.

Neither man spoke for a while. Instead, they gazed introspectively at the dying embers in the grate. Eventually, Midnight put down his drink and held his head in his hands, shaking it and muttering behind his palms.

"I failed, Giles. I failed them all. Perhaps this is how it was meant to be. Everything was fine and dandy when it was just you, Mrs P and myself. It does no good to let people in, Giles. I have ruined Gredge's life. He has lost his home, his position, his respect, and possibly his mind! I failed to protect him from all the baggage that comes with being acquainted with me. I have made my daughter hate me by pushing away the people she truly loves, and now... now I am to abandon her to travel halfway around the world with no notion of when I might return." Midnight paused in order to gain control of the quiver in his voice.

"Perhaps I am meant to be alone. Someone, no... some*thing* like me should not be allowed to love. I am a dark stain, a blight on the happiness of others." Midnight's voice cracked as he spoke.

Unable to contain his despair, he launched the bottle of brandy and its remaining contents into the fire. It smashed, and the embers flared as they came into contact with the alcohol.

"I have been thinking, Giles. Why is it that my dark powers are stronger than the light? There must be a reason why objects connected with bad spirits, like the mask, always seem to find their way to me. Father never did manage to figure out where my powers came from or why I was born so." He tugged at his shirt until an area of skin on his chest was exposed, revealing the oddly shaped birthmark that had always been labelled as his 'Devil's mark'. "And then, there's this! I have never truly questioned my existence before, Giles. Father always maintained that I was born to protect the weak and vulnerable, but how is it that those very same people I am meant to protect suffer greatly at my hands?"

Giles took another sip of brandy before answering. "Your father had many secrets, Master Midnight. The cube being one of them. After your mother's death, Josiah would spend every spare moment he had in that library—" He pointed at the ceiling. "—reading and reading from sundown to sunrise, scribbling notes and ideas. He rarely discussed them with me, of course. I was told only what I needed to know, and I have had the very great privilege to watch you grow from a young, impetuous child into the man that you are today: a man of impeccable morals who judges others not by their wealth or social standing but by their actions; a man who fights for justice, who builds hospitals for those who need care, who gives money to worthy charities that help the people of his city; a man who sacrificed his need for privacy to provide stability and a loving home for an orphaned girl, a groom, and a young maid."

Midnight flinched, his gut tightening at the mention of Laura.

"Sir, it matters not what you were born with—dark or light. It matters not why you were born or how. The only thing that matters is *how* you use those powers. Whether the eventual outcome is how you imagined or not, your intentions are always good and are always conducted with love in your heart." Giles shifted forwards in his seat to look directly into Midnight's watery eyes. "You are a good man. Whether you see it or not, it is the truth. People will come in and out of your life as they choose. It is the ones who come back to you who are truly meant to be there. Do not despair. I have a feeling that we will see Mr Gredge again as soon as he is ready. As for Miss Carter," Giles added perceptively, "who knows? She has her own path to walk, and only she knows where she is headed."

"Polly is so angry with me, but she is young; she does not understand how these things work—or cannot work, in this case. How can I explain it to her, Giles?"

The old butler smiled. "The little miss will forgive you. She adores you, but she is grieving, too, for the loss of loved ones. Give her time to process things. She's a bright young madam, and she will come around. Mark my words."

The two men regarded each other, and something unspoken passed between them: a long-held mutual respect and understanding born from secrecy, and nurtured over a lifetime of loss and survival—one young and lonely Lord of the Realm, and his butler, his confidant, his friend.

Midnight realised suddenly that he had been mourning the loss of what he had thought was his only friend in Arthur, and yet, here sat his oldest friend and greatest ally of all. An eon apart, both in age and in material means, but equals as men. Between them stood a bond of friendship and loyalty that none could break or could ever compare to, and, for that, Midnight thought himself the luckiest man alive.

31

MERITON
MARCH 3RD 1863

ЯⅡR

A solitary candle burned in the basement, casting its dancing light against the struggling shadows that threatened to suffocate the flickering flame. Its dim glow reflected in the many mirrors that adorned the walls of Midnight's secret room.

There were only a few precious hours left before he set sail across the ocean, Miss Agnes Carmichael in tow. It was a journey any ordinary man might make, but he was no ordinary man, and these were no ordinary times. In days past he had fallen into a melancholic despair, questioning his very existence and purpose. Now, he stood before a mirror and looked deep into himself.

"No more hiding, Midnight." He spoke softly but firmly to his reflection. "It is time to accept who you are. You were born this way for a reason, and even if you do not fully understand why, there is no point in hiding the truth from yourself anymore. Look at who you truly are and embrace it."

He closed his eyes and breathed deeply. When he looked again in the mirror, his real face stared mockingly back at him. He was not shocked by the way he looked. He had seen it many times before, but he had always had to disguise it, bury it deep behind the smokescreen he created to fit in. Now, he forced himself to examine every inch, every glorious gory detail of his half-skeletal appearance.

He cast his eyes over the human half first, the familiar line of his jaw, the bridge of his nose, the defined brow and deep-set crystal blue eye that flashed in the candlelight. His light half was the one he presented to the world. It was the side of him that balanced out the sinister shadows that squirmed inside of him, always baying to break free.

The dark side of him lay secretly submerged beneath the surface, waiting, reminding him of that blissful pain of acceptance. Raising a hand to his face, he touched his fingers to the protruding, bare cheekbone and hollow eye socket that was presented to him in the mirror. He felt the flesh, and skin beneath his fingertips—he was still whole. This dark visage was just another part of him, as much as his hand or arm or his smile was.

He *was* different to other men but that no longer mattered. What mattered was how he chose to live his life and how he chose to behave towards others. The monster who stared back at him was not a monster at all. Exactly what he was, Midnight was determined to find out.

He would begin where his father had left off. There were boxes and boxes of notebooks locked away in the attic. He had an entire library at his disposal, money to allow him to travel the entire globe if need be, to help him discover his truth. Acceptance had to begin with truth, however dark it may prove to be. Of course, he could not put this plan into action just yet. He had to accompany Miss Carmichael across an ocean and deliver her to her family safely. Then, he would have to wait for a return voyage home.

Home, what did that even mean now with Gredge and

Laura gone, Agnes leaving, and his daughter still locked away in her room in her self-imposed isolation? There had been times in the last few years where he had lamented those days of solitude alongside his two long-suffering staff, yet now, he felt a sense of loss that he had not experienced since his father's passing. There was a love for and a strong need to have those people close to him once more, a need for control that could not be fulfilled. And so, he would focus that need on discovering the secrets of his past in order to move on into his future, whatever that may be.

32

ROYAL DOCKS

MARCH 3RD 1863

ЯⅢR

They stood on the deck of *The City of New York* as she was about to set sail, surrounded by hundreds of other passengers who stood side by side, three to four people dense at the railing, waving their goodbyes. Shouts of 'Bon Voyage!' and 'Don't forget to write!" came in droves from the dock. Midnight found his own little group in the crowd below. Mrs P was waving her handkerchief frantically, then intermittently using it to dab the tears from her eyes. Giles, who stood proud and stoic, raised a hand in farewell. And then there was Polly. She had her face buried in Charlie's coat, her small shoulders heaving. Midnight's throat tightened. She had come to the docks to see them off and had said a tearful farewell to her governess, Agnes, but ignored her father when he had attempted to embrace her.

The ship's horn blew loud and clear to signal their imminent departure. As the liner's chimney's billowed and the great metal hulk began to pull away from the dock, people gradually began to dissipate from the deck, eager to search out their cabins and settle in.

"If you don't mind, sir, I think I will go and unpack," Agnes said.

"Of course. Do what you must," he replied without taking his eyes from the small figure that still clung tightly to Charlie.

The ship began to turn away from the stragglers who continued to wave and shout from the shore; some had started to walk away. Midnight stood his ground and kept watching. Just as the gap between the ship and the shore widened, the figure broke away and ran along the dock towards the ship, ribbons and curls bouncing madly behind her.

"Polly!" Midnight shouted and made his way quickly along the railing at the ship's stern. He leaned as far over the rails as he dared in attempt to hear what she was shouting.

Polly's hand was cupped to her mouth, her mutilated left arm raised high in the air, waving madly.

"Darling, I cannot hear you!" he yelled, pointing to his ear.

The girl stamped her feet and shouted again. A fortuitous wind carried her desperate cries, and his heart skipped with joy and relief. "Papa! Papa, I love you! I'm sorry. Don't leave me? Papa! Come back!"

"Darling girl, I love you too. I promise you; I will be home soon!"

They stayed and watched each other grow smaller and further away until each was a distant, unrecognisable dot on the horizon.

It was strange, he thought, how one did not realise the value of something until it was no longer available. He made his mind up then to watch the sunrise in the east every day of his voyage, for east was where his family—the people he loved the most—waited for him to come back to them.

EPILOGUE
CRAWLEY MANOR - MARCH 3RD 1863

ℛ|ℛ

"Is this everything?" Gredge asked as he took the heavy box of books and items from Elldy and carried them into the library at Crawley Manor.

"Anything and everything I could think of," she replied, beginning to unpack one of the many boxes piled high on the large oak table.

"We are going to be very busy by the looks of it," Gredge said and sighed.

"It will be worth it in the end... if we can help him."

"Are you sure you're right about all of this?" Gredge swept a hand across the room. "I mean, if you are wrong, he is going to be extremely angry with the both of us."

"He will be extremely angry with the both of us regardless of whether I am right or wrong," Elldy huffed. "And I *am* right. I am sure of it." She stopped unpacking and turned to face him. "Arthur, if anyone should understand the value of truth, it should be you, after everything you are coming to terms with, everything you have been through. Besides, we *all* deserve to know exactly what we might be up against. Don't you agree?"

Gredge shrugged and drew his smoking jacket tighter around himself. "I suppose so. Right, then. Where do we begin?" he asked, drawing a hand across his chin and tugging his moustache.

Elldy placed her hands on her hips and said, "We begin at the beginning. With this!" Opening a small, innocuous-looking box, Elldy reached inside and pulled out the wooden cube, engraved with Viking bind runes that had previously belonged to the enigmatic Josephine Gunn, the cube that had once glowed bright blue with magic.

ACKNOWLEDGMENTS

Before I reel off my list of 'thank yous', I first need to acknowledge my own efforts in completing this book. I began plotting this story back in late 2019 with the notion of publishing it within six months. In January 2020 I was diagnosed with breast cancer and my whole life was put on hold. Once my surgery and treatments finished, I was determined to finish this project. I had a story to tell, and nothing would get in my way. I'm here giving myself a congratulatory pat on the back for managing what I set out to do despite the horrendous side effects of chemotherapy, radiotherapy, and the physical and mental hurdles I am still working to overcome. Go me! You did okay, lady.

Of course, I would not have achieved any of this without incredible support from my husband, and my parents. You always have my back and I love you all dearly. Thank you.

To Lorna and Laura, where would I be without you?

Gratitude is also extended to the wonderful team of superheroes at Hudson Indie Ink. You are more than my publisher; you are my book family. I cannot thank you all enough for the support, patience, and continued encouragement you have shown. Thank you for believing in me, you have shown me the path to the stars and helped me to shine.

Lastly, to the people who live in my world with me - my readers, you are the reason I strive to do better, to work hard at producing stories that you want to read, and characters you come to know and love. Thank you from the bottom of my heart for loving my words and the worlds I create.

ABOUT THE AUTHOR

C. L. Monaghan is a self-confessed Scotophile living in the Kingdom of Fife. Writer of award-winning Gothic and historical mystery, and paranormal romance. Lover of hairy coos and red squirrels. Explorer of ancient ruined castles and beautiful glens. You can discover more about her and her books at: www.clmonaghan.com

 facebook.com/Joesbookbar

 twitter.com/MonaghanAuthor

 instagram.com/clairemonaghan73

ALSO BY C. L. MONAGHAN

The Immaginario Duet

Immaginario

Andato

The Midnight Gunn Series

The Hollows

The Barghest

The Draugr

Steel Petals: An Anthology of Poems

OTHER AUTHORS AT HUDSON INDIE INK

Paranormal Romance/Urban Fantasy

Sloane Murphy

Stephanie Hudson

Xen Randell

C. L. Monaghan

Sorcha Dawn

Kia Carrington-Russell

Sci-fi/Fantasy

Devin Hanson

Crime/Action

Blake Hudson

Mike Gomes

Contemporary Romance

Gemma Weir

Elodie Colt

Ann B. Harrison

9 781913 769758